From the beloved author of
To Kill a Mockingbird
and *Go Set a Watchman* comes
The Land of Sweet Forever

A teenage girl harbours a secret; another is given a pair of binoculars which she uses to spy on her community; a postgraduate student in Manhattan receives a dark surprise from her neighbour; and a young woman returns home to Maycomb, Alabama, to find that everything has changed – these and more are the never-before-seen stories by Harper Lee, published here for the first time.

Before Lee was a literary legend, she was a movie-goer, a scholar, and a New York City transplant who wrote wryly comic and acutely observed essays that appeared in top magazines. The second section of The Land of Sweet Forever features her later non-fiction, offering reflections on a wide range of themes, including equality, travel, love, fiction, art, and what it means to live an engaged and creative life.

Insightful and illuminating, this is an indispensable collection of short fiction, essays and magazine pieces for devoted fans and new readers alike. This edition features an introduction by Casey Cep, Lee's appointed biographer, and an essay by Dr Edwin Lee Conner, nephew of Harper Lee.

The Land of Sweet Forever

ALSO BY HARPER LEE

To Kill a Mockingbird

Go Set a Watchman

Harper Lee

The Land of Sweet Forever

HUTCHINSON
HEINEMANN

HUTCHINSON HEINEMANN

UK | USA | Canada | Ireland | Australia
India | New Zealand | South Africa

Hutchinson Heinemann is part of the Penguin Random House group of companies
whose addresses can be found at global.penguinrandomhouse.com

Penguin Random House UK,
One Embassy Gardens, 8 Viaduct Gardens, London SW11 7BW

penguin.co.uk

Penguin
Random House
UK

First published 2025

001

In preparing this book, the Publisher has made every effort to remain true to the original typewritten texts of the short stories, which had been prepared by the author as ready to present for publication in a periodical. The only changes made were corrections of minor typographical errors or misspellings.

Printed and bound in Great Britain by Clays Ltd, Elcograf S.p.A.

The authorised representative in the EEA is Penguin Random House Ireland,
Morrison Chambers, 32 Nassau Street, Dublin D02 YH68

A CIP catalogue record for this book is available from the British Library

ISBN: 978–1–529–15566–2

Penguin Random House is committed to a sustainable future for our business, our readers and our planet. This book is made from Forest Stewardship Council® certified paper.

FSC
www.fsc.org
MIX
Paper | Supporting responsible forestry
FSC® C018179

CONTENTS

INTRODUCTION

by Casey Cep

WHEN *TO KILL A MOCKINGBIRD* was published in the summer of 1960, it seemed to have sprung from nowhere, like an Alabamian Athena: a perfectly formed novel from an unknown Southern writer without any evident precedent or antecedent. The book somehow managed to be both urgently of its time and instantly timeless, addressing the era's most turbulent issues, from the Civil Rights Movement to the Sexual Revolution, while also speaking in the register of the eternal, from the moral awakening of children and the abiding love of families to the frictions between the self and society.

But no writer is without influences and aspirations: Harper Lee had, of course, come from somewhere and worked tremendously hard to become someone. It was only because she did not like talking about herself that her origins seemed so mysterious, and inevitably, the better *To Kill a Mockingbird* did—becoming a bestseller and then winning a Pulitzer Prize, selling a million copies and then ten million and then forty million—the more theories and rumors rushed in to fill her silence. In the years after the book came out, the public image of Lee swung between two of her beloved characters: She was either the living incarnation of her feisty, tomboyish heroine Jean Louise "Scout" Finch or, in her seeming reclusiveness, a version of that shy shadow figure, Arthur "Boo" Radley. Absent answers from the author herself, who she really was and how she became a writer were questions that sidestepped the usual form of biography and moved into the realm of mythology.

How thrilling, then, to encounter this time capsule from the start of Lee's career: a collection of some of her earliest short stories, appearing here in print for the first time, which help explain how the little girl from South Alabama Avenue turned herself into a bestselling author who enchanted generations of readers around the world. Drafted in the decade before *To Kill a Mockingbird*, after Lee had first moved to New York City in 1949, these stories, the first eight pieces in this volume, feature some of the characters and settings she would soon make famous and reveal some of the contradictions and conflicts she would spend her life trying to resolve.

Nelle Harper Lee was born on April 28, 1926, the last of Amasa Coleman Lee and Frances Cunningham Finch's four children. Fifteen years younger than her oldest sibling, she grew up feeling as if she had her own private childhood in the small town of Monroeville, Alabama, some hundred miles south of Montgomery and a hundred light-years from Manhattan. Because her siblings were so much older, she watched them one by one fulfill the dreams of their parents: a respectable legal career alongside their father for her sister Alice; a loving marriage and homemaker's life for her sister Louise; heroic military service in the Second World War for her brother, Edwin. For a long while, it seemed as if Lee would be the family's one great disappointment: She dropped out of the University of Alabama a semester shy of graduation, fleeing to the disreputable North and abandoning the law degree that would have allowed her father to add an *s* to the family firm's shingle. But while A.C. Lee and Daughters was not meant to be and Lee did not become a lawyer, she did eventually create the most admired attorney in America.

Although Lee never formally studied creative writing, she spent her years in Tuscaloosa teaching herself to write. She had a recurring column in the college newspaper, *The Crimson White*, and contributed sketches to the student humor magazine, the *Rammer Jammer*, which she eventually edited. Even then, her roving curiosity and intellectual range were evident on the page—in a review of recent British films, a parody of Shakespeare, a send-up of the registrar, a roast of the rural newspaper her father edited and owned—and her byline always marked the entrance to a briar patch: What followed was prickly and irreverent, like Nelle herself, as she was known back then. A Chi Omega who corrected her sorority sisters whenever they mispronounced words, Lee wore blue jeans and Bermuda shorts at a time when women were discouraged from wearing anything but dresses, cursed more than the crew of the USS *Enterprise*, and once scandalized the entire campus by smoking a cigar on the hood of a car in the homecoming parade.

Lee knew approximately one person in New York City when she moved there at age twenty-three, but what a person he was: Truman Capote, who had spent some of his childhood living next door to her, and who would later serve as the model for the puny, puckish Charles Baker "Dill" Harris in her novel. The budding authors felt like "apart people," as Capote later put it, already able to read years before their peers, playing with language the way others did dolls and footballs. The pair conspired with each other to write adventures, tall tales, and verses of the sort they so liked reading, from the Bobbsey Twins to Beowulf and the Rover Boys to Rudyard Kipling, clattering away at the typewriter that A.C. Lee had given his bookish youngest daughter.

In lieu of college, Capote had gone directly to work as a copy boy at *The New Yorker.* A few years later, Lee landed her own job in publishing, although at nowhere near so storied a publication: While Capote had scandalized editor Harold Ross by wearing a cape and annoyed Robert Frost by disrupting one of his poetry readings, Lee faced the drudgery of proofreading conference calendars and education news for the monthly magazine of the American School Publishing Corporation, a trade rag called *The School Executive*. Eventually she left that day job for another, this one as an airline reservation clerk, which was less literary but theoretically more glamorous. The same could not be said of the rest of her life back then: Around the edges of her nine-to-five work, she lived off peanut butter sandwiches while drafting stories at a desk she made for herself with two old apple crates and a door she found in the basement of her building.

Writing on that shaky surface, Lee gradually steadied her hand. "I do believe that my greatest talent lies in creative writing," she wrote to her family, confidingly and confidently, "and I do believe I can make a living at it." Like so many aspiring authors, she initially turned to that family and her own early life for material, and the first three stories in this collection shuffle through a series of young narrators to explore the social mores, tiny transgressions, and moral confusion of what, in one of her later stories, she so beautifully calls "childhood's secret society." The stakes of "The Water Tank," "The Binoculars," and "The Pinking Shears," all written before she turned thirty, are profoundly circumscribed—the approval of one's parents and the acceptance of one's peers—and the antagonists aren't very grand either: teachers, siblings, schoolyard cliques.

The next three stories, by contrast, are all set in New York, with adult narrators, and one senses Lee trying to keep up with the Salingers and Cheevers. Still, that trio—"A Roomful of Kibble," "The Viewers and the Viewed," and "This Is Show Business?"—does show her moving beyond incident and toward plot, while simultaneously experimenting with different narrative voices. They take the not-quite-experimental form of a comic-tragic monologue about a should-have-been-medicated friend, the heckling banter of an Upper East Side movie audience, and the conversations of two near-strangers in the Aristotelian theater of an idling automobile. People are often surprised to learn that Lee spent most of her life in New York City, borrowing books from the Society Library, taking in exhibits at the Frick, and trekking out to Queens to go to Mets games, and there's something startling and sublime about reading our great balladeer of small-town culture on the frustrations of finding a place to park in Manhattan, sounding for all the world like a Southern Seinfeld.

Characters taken directly from Lee's own life appear throughout these tales. One sports her own nickname, Dody; others bear the names of her siblings, Edwin, Alice, and Louise; some are thinly disguised or entirely undisguised versions of her friends, including future Monroeville mayor Anne Hines. Even her brother's eventual wife appears by name: Sara Ann McCall, who, as a little girl, played the ham in the real-life agricultural products parade Lee would later borrow for a pivotal scene at the end of *To Kill a Mockingbird*. Lee's oldest sister, Alice, known to the whole family as "Bear," is here transformed ever so slightly into "Doe," but remains instantly recognizable despite the name: "She loved only three things in this world," Lee writes, "the study and practice of law, camellias, and the Methodist Church."

Like hospitality or lane cakes, names are a Southern specialty, and Lee already had a fine ear for them, making them up with great gusto whenever she didn't poach them. We meet in these stories one Eddie May Ousley, a "failure" who was held back in school; a pair of teachers named Miss Busey and Miss Turnipseed; and the preacher Brother Q W Tatum, no periods after the initials, please, with his near minyan of nine children, Haniel, Job, Habakkuk, Matrid, Jezebel, Mary, Emmanuel, and a set of twins, Hosea and Hosannah.

The name for which Harper Lee is most well-known first appears in "The Pinking Shears," when we meet "little Jean Louie," a third-grade troublemaker who is rather awkwardly missing her *s*. For the time being, the more familiar "Louise," which was Lee's middle sister's given name, is stuck elsewhere, on a girl with the surname Finley—a disgraced grade-schooler whose pregnancy scandalizes her entire sixth-grade class in "The Water Tank." In both stories, young women struggle with the expectations of their mothers, fathers, and neighbors, though Lee's tone is less gloomy than gleeful, as befits these miniature comedies of manners. The narrator of "The Water Tank" spends the whole story worrying that she's about to have a baby, because shortly after getting her first period, she hugged a boy whose pants were down. In "The Pinking Shears," Jean Louie Finch, confounded by gendered grooming expectations, is punished for cutting the wild, waist-length hair of a classmate over the objections of that girl's tyrannical, Old-Testament father.

By the last of the stories that appear in this collection, Miss Finch has officially become "Jean Louise," though she's not yet Scout. Those who knew Harper Lee best all summon her blistering intellect, and one of the pleasures of this final story is seeing that brilliance unleashed on the page—a story so dense with allusions that readers are not even expected to understand them. The title, "The Land of Sweet Forever," comes from a hymn, and much of the plot, as if borrowed from Thackeray or Trollope, concerns itself, hilariously, with hymnody. Now a grown adult, Jean Louise is thoroughly conversant in lesser Anglican theologians, preposterously opinionated about the proper pacing of the Doxology, and peevish about alterations to tradition, mock-seriously complaining that "our brethren in the northland are not content merely with the Supreme Court's activities: they are now trying to change our hymns on us."

Lee is funny and formidably smart on the simultaneous comfort and claustrophobia of returning as an adult to one's childhood home, or one's childhood anything, even church. By the time she wrote "The Land of Sweet Forever," she was well-versed in such returns, having already made a great many of them. Two years after she moved to New York, in the summer of 1951, her father had called from the Vaughan Memorial Hospital in Selma to say that her mother had been diagnosed with cancer of the liver and lungs. Before Lee could even arrange for travel home, A.C. called again, this time to say that Frances had died of a cardiac episode only a day after being diagnosed; it was only thanks to the airline where Lee still worked that she could even make it back in time for the service.

Six weeks later, that first dreadful phone call was followed by another, this one informing her that her beloved brother, Edwin, the inspiration for Jem, had died of a brain aneurysm at the air force base where he was stationed in Montgomery, leaving behind a wife and two young children. Lee flew home again, her already considerable grief and shock now overflowing. She was just twenty-five years old, but capturing her childhood had never felt more urgent, partly because, as she describes in "The Cat's Meow," her father and oldest sister soon sold the family home where she'd been born and raised, moving into a more modern house on the other side of town. While Alice continued to commute the short distance from there to their law office on the courthouse square, A.C. stayed home and convalesced: bereft, riddled with arthritis, and soon troubled by cardiac issues of his own.

The move did not help the pair of homebodies escape the ghosts of South Alabama Avenue, and Lee, too, was haunted by memories of her mother, her brother, and the world as it had existed before they died. She worried over her father and returned home often to help Alice with his care. She also began writing stories that attempted to reconcile her chosen home with her childhood one, merging the subjectivity of her Manhattan stories with the setting of her Monroeville stories, a kind of integrative work she was attempting both on and off the page.

At the time, Lee's politics were still taking shape, especially when it came to the era's most pressing moral concerns. The long struggle for civil rights was unfolding all across the nation but most contentiously in the Deep South, and like so many white Americans, Harper Lee wasn't quite sure what to make of it. Her hometown was strictly segregated, with schools, churches, and restaurants divided by race; her own father had written newspaper editorials opposing federal antilynching laws, defending the conviction of the so-called Scottsboro Boys, who were falsely accused of raping two white women, and cautioning that a national education department might enforce the desegregation of schools.

Lee's emerging political sensibility diverged from that of her father, but it remained to be seen by how much. In college, she had written some about the horrors of racial violence and made herself comfortable among the radicals on the student newspaper, although it would be nearly twenty years before Vivian Malone and James Hood bravely integrated the University of Alabama. Upon arriving in Manhattan, however, she settled into a society more diverse than any she'd ever known, and she joked about joining the NAACP. Even her Southern friends there were entirely reconstructed, and she quickly adjusted to integrated life, including by developing a sense of moral superiority that she brought home with her to Alabama. "I refrained from reminding Doe that for the past seven years I had lived in New York City," Lee writes in "The Cat's Meow," "where among other things more than eight million people enjoy the benefits of democracy."

That story—submitted in early 1957, three years after the Supreme Court decided *Brown v. Board of Education* and a few months before President Eisenhower would sign the first civil rights legislation since Reconstruction—tackles race relations directly. In it, a pair of small-town siblings, clearly Lee and her older sister Alice, who scarcely left Monroeville except to attend college in Montgomery and law school in Birmingham, find themselves confounded by their gardener, Arthur, "a Yankee Negro" whose horticultural talents and criminal past alternately arouse their prejudice, curiosity, and pity.

Lee was prescient in recognizing that the Civil Rights Movement was not just an abstract crusade for justice, but a series of direct confrontations between neighbors; its success depended on changing policy and also on changing the nature and terms of real relationships. That conviction would be beautifully realized on the page in *To Kill a Mockingbird*, which helps explain why the novel was so successful, not just commercially but also culturally: Atticus, that exemplar of moral courage for his children, became a moral example for readers as well, a reminder that every human interaction presents the opportunity to obey our better angels.

In "The Cat's Meow," though, Lee hasn't even sorted out her relationship to her family of origin, much less her feelings about the fight for social justice. At one point, when the narrator of the story finally admits her own discomfort with Arthur, the gardener, she confesses: "Doe said it was because I couldn't adjust myself to an emancipated Negro at such close quarters and that it proved no matter how long I lived away from home I would always be from Maycomb, Alabama, to which I preserved an uncharacteristic silence, for Doe was a deep-water segregationist, I was not, and the last thing I wanted was a row which would separate me from the only family I had left. I suppose a lot of people like me have mastered the first lesson of living at home these days:

if you don't agree with what you hear, place your tongue between your teeth and bite hard." Ultimately, that story is unsettling because, in its final lines, the narrator follows her own advice: opting for what could be silent condemnation, but could just as easily be read as silent complicity.

Throughout her longhand drafts and typescripts of these stories, Lee left editing marks—many of them the flyspecks of strike-throughs and substitutions that one expects of any work in progress, but some of them more significant revisions. On an early page of "The Water Tank," in red pen, she replaced "Monroe County" with "Maiben County," a first stab at making her hometown of Monroeville into the kind of fictional world in which moral transformation might be possible. By "The Cat's Meow," Maiben has officially become Maycomb, soon to be one of the most storied small towns in American literature.

Another kind of map emerges from these manuscripts, too. Because she was sending the stories out to places she hoped might publish them—little magazines like *Tomorrow* and literary mainstays like *Harper's Bazaar* and *The New Yorker*, whose rejection letter she saved—Lee added her address to the title page of each one, so that, collectively, they trace her early, frenetic years in Manhattan: first a cold-water flat at 1540 Second Avenue on the Upper East Side, then a room at the Wolcott Hotel in Midtown, where Edith Wharton and Mark Twain once lived; then a third-floor walk-up at 1539 York Avenue, where she paid some twenty dollars a month for five years, and where she wrote both *Go Set a Watchman* and *To Kill a Mockingbird*.

For a long time, these stories were just tantalizing titles typed on a smudged and stained index card in the archives of her agents, Annie Laurie Williams and Maurice Crain. One of the stories still has an address label from Crain's agency affixed to its first page. "Lee, Nelle Harper, Miss," some long-ago secretary noted, dropped off some manuscripts a few days after Thanksgiving in 1956, then retrieved them a week later. "Author is a nice little Southern gal from Alabama," Crain himself had noted in an agency memo: "Says No, Ma'am, Yes, Ma'am." None of the stories noted in the files were published, and for decades scholars and biographers alike wondered what had become of them. Four of them finally appear here; together with the other four, they were found in the last of the novelist's New York City apartments, this one at 433 East Eighty-Second Street, where she moved the year *To Kill a Mockingbird* was published and where she lived another four decades until a stroke sent her home to Alabama for good.

Happily for posterity, Lee was a pack rat: When that apartment was cleaned out, there amidst piles of her correspondence and practically every pay stub, telephone bill, and canceled check ever issued to her, were her notebooks and manuscripts, including the eight stories and the eight nonfiction pieces collected here. The essays explore some of the same themes as her fiction, offering reflections on childhood, family, friendship, Southern history, the life of the mind, and the moral status, such as it was, of America. Unlike the fiction, the nonfiction was all previously published: Lee wrote for *Vogue*; contributed to a cookbook alongside Lillian Hellman, William Styron, and Marianne Moore; riffed on her favorite historian; profiled her celebrity friends Gregory Peck and Truman Capote; and told *O Magazine* the story of how she learned to read. Slightly cantankerous by then in her role as literary elder stateswoman, she struck the same wry tone as in her undergraduate "Caustic Comment" newspaper columns: "Oprah," she wrote, "can you imagine curling up in bed to read a computer? Weeping for Anna Karenina and being terrified by Hannibal Lecter, entering the heart of darkness with Mistah Kurtz, having Holden Caulfield ring you up—some things should happen on soft pages, not cold metal."

These essays make clear that, in the decades after *To Kill a Mockingbird*, Lee enjoyed the career she'd always wanted, even if her fans never got from her the career they expected. Her masterpiece was adapted into a wildly successful and award-winning film, has never been out of print, and was translated into dozens of languages, defying boundaries and borders and cementing itself both on school syllabi and on the shelves of millions of households around the world. But she never wrote the sequel or second novel that so many of her admirers yearned for, and when, at the age of eighty-nine, she did finally publish another book, it was *Go Set a Watchman*, the first one she'd ever written, originally submitted to publishers the same year as "The Binoculars."

"I am more of a rewriter than a writer," Lee once said, explaining that she generally worked through at least three drafts of any given piece of writing. As that suggests, she was devoted to her work and, at least at first, strikingly disciplined about it. "I generally get a good day's work done every day," she wrote in a letter to one of her sisters in October 1950: "If I paid myself overtime, I'd be rich." She went on to describe a typical writing day during this era:

> From around noon, work on the first draft. By dinnertime, I've usually put my idea down. I then stop for a sandwich or a full meal, depending on whether I've got to think more about the story or just finish it. After dinner, I work on a second draft, which involves sometimes tearing the story up and putting it together again in an entirely different way, or just keeping at it until everything is like I want it. Then I retype it on white paper, conforming to rules of manuscript preparation, and run out & mail it. That sounds simple, but sometimes I have worked through the night on one; usually I end up around two or three in the morning.

Some of that hard work is visible here, not only on the physical manuscripts themselves, but upon comparing the early stories to her published novels. "The Binoculars," for instance, was abridged and adapted into the pedagogical standoff in the second chapter of *To Kill a Mockingbird*, when Scout's first-grade teacher gets frustrated with her for knowing how to read. Similarly, "The Land of Sweet Forever" became a set piece in the seventh chapter of *Go Set a Watchman*, when Scout returns home to Maycomb from New York City.

But that title story is also repurposed, less obviously, in *To Kill a Mockingbird*, when Scout and Jem accompany their Black maid to First Purchase African Methodist Episcopal Church. Built by former slaves, the worship space was their "first purchase" after emancipation; largely illiterate and lacking additional money for hymnals, the congregants sang by call and response, which they are still doing generations later when Calpurnia takes the Finch children to Sunday services. "There's a land beyond the river," her son Zeebo sings, leading the chorus, "that we call the sweet forever." Lee, now at the height of her novelistic powers, found her way into an unfamiliar sanctuary, bringing her central characters there as well, a rare moment of integration in a world rigidly divided by race. A hymn previously deployed for comic effect here becomes a common language and a common hope. Lee writes gorgeously that the cantor's voice was "like the rumble of distant artillery," and from this side of history, readers know what troops will follow, all those brave men and women who fought for justice and equality on this side of heaven.

It takes enormous patience and unerring instincts to refine a scrap of story into something so keen and moving. Between the title pages and her literary agency's records, we know that Lee spent seven years writing and revising these short stories and then, after they caught her agent's eye and he encouraged her to try for something longer, spent another three years turning those stories into chapters, and those chapters into novels—first *Go Set a Watchman* and then *To Kill a Mockingbird*.

All this would have taken even longer had it not been for an extraordinary gift Lee received, which she describes in one of the best essays collected here, "Christmas to Me." Among her closest friends in New York were a husband and wife, Michael and Joy Brown, who had long championed her career. It was Michael Brown, a celebrated lyricist and composer, who had first introduced Lee to her literary agents, shortly before Thanksgiving of 1956, and he and his wife both delighted in her stories and in the remarkable letters she sent them from back home in Alabama—small masterpieces of the epistolary form, specific and funny, sociologically astute, surprisingly tender.

The Browns and Lee were in the habit of spending Christmas together, and they had developed a tradition of trying to see which of them could give the least expensive yet most outrageous gift. That year, Lee had spent thirty-five cents on a portrait of an obscure English cleric for Michael and acquired a bargain copy of the complete works of a slightly less obscure British aristocrat for Joy. When it came time for the Browns to present the novelist with her gift, they pointed to an envelope on their tree. It seemed appropriately modest from the outside, but in fact, they had radically broken with tradition: Inside was a note that read, "You have one year off from your job to write whatever you please. Merry Christmas." That month, and nearly every month thereafter for the next year, they wrote her a check for a hundred dollars, five times her rent, insisting they wanted nothing in return.

For decades, that gift has seemed shocking, an act so generous it bordered on the preposterous. Now, though, with the rediscovery of these stories, we get to see what Lee's friends saw all those years ago: a lawyer father not yet named Atticus but already modeling high-mindedness and teaching his single-digit children civil procedure; a small-town versifier who feuds with the local newspaper printer over the propriety and theological permissibility of publishing obituaries for cows; a daughter of the South trying to map its mores onto her own emerging morals; glimpse after glimpse after glimpse of genius. No wonder the Browns gave Harper Lee that gift; it was no more lavish than her own.

which she cultivated silently for three months, and its Methodist Church, where she went every Sunday and sang hymns at the top of her voice.

There is nothing like a blood-curdling hymn to make one feel at home. All sense of isolation withers and dies in the presence of some two hundred sinners earnestly requesting to be plunged beneath a red, redeeming flood. While offering to the Lord the results of Mr. Cowper's hallucination, or declaring it was Love that lifted her, Jean Louise ~~could~~ shared the warmness that prevails among diverse individuals who climb into the same boat for one hour each week.

She was totally unprepared for what happened immediately after collection on the Sunday before the Friday she was due to return to New York. Maycomb Methodists sing what they call The Doxology in lieu of the minister praying over the collection plate to spare him the rigors involved in inventing yet another prayer, since by that time he has uttered three healthy invocations. From the time of her earliest ecclesiastical recollection, Maycomb Methodists had sung The Doxology in one way and in one way only:

A page from the original typescript of the story "The Land of Sweet Forever"

Stories

The
WATER TANK

FROM WHERE SHE SAT IN the schoolyard, Abbie thought she could see sky and toasted fields shimmer where they touched. Too hot for townball. She groaned and stretched her legs out stiff in the yellow grass, wondering why her big toes were so big—out of proportion to the rest of her feet. She was not a child one wished to reach out and touch: the nails in her blunt fingers were ragged, several red scars on the coarse knuckle-skin matched those on her knees. The brown hair at her forehead was scraggly where bangs had grown too long, and her oversize eyes were set deeply in the skull, so heavy-lidded as to make them seem half open. They called her sluggish-looking.

A bulky clump of girls sprawled around her, barefooted and dressed in faded cotton prints. They were Group Two of the sixth grade, fifteen- and sixteen-year-olds who chopped cotton half the year and learned what they could the rest: thick-ankled girls with red faces, shiny pink hands and parched hair. This year Abbie's companions were Group Two; the crude farm speech and wisdom that alienated them from the other town children fascinated her. Unwittingly Abbie gave in return what their parents wanted for them: a town friend who would go to the University and someday marry a dentist or a lawyer, or at least return home and be a secretary in the Maiben County Bank.

The largest girl hissed the breath out of her lungs and crawled toward Abbie. "Move over," she said. "Ground's so hot I can't sit on it."

As Maybelle pulled herself up on the grey stone bench, Abbie smelled Hoyt's Cologne-and-sweat. "Better not let Miss Nash get a whiff of you, Hawkins," she said.

Maybelle snorted. "Only reason she told us not to wear it's because she's after Raymond Walters herself." Raymond was the oldest and tallest boy in Maiben County Elementary: seventeen and six feet. Group Two came to school that year with frizzled hair and compacts, which Miss Nash thought she had put a stop to immediately. "The younger children," she had said in one of her numerous private talks. "They all look up to you older girls, and you have a great influence on them for good or evil. Let's make it good, shall we?"

"She can't do anything to me," said Maybelle belligerently. "I'd smack her in the can with a grubbin' hoe." The girls snickered.

"Well, better stay away from her today. Saw her eating that chalky stuff again, so she's got indigestion."

"Miss Nash can go feel herself. Say, Ab, hear about Louise Finley? Everybody was talkin' about it on the bus this morning." Maybelle's blue eyes gleamed.

"Naw, who's she?"

Maybelle waved a pink finger toward the high-school building. "She's in ninth grade. Mildred's big sister."

Abbie nodded. Mildred Finley was a pop-eyed fourth-grader from Mexia who caused a sensation the first day of school by not knowing how to flush a toilet. "Yeah? What about her?" asked Abbie.

"Well—hey everybody, wake up! Yawl heard about Louise Finley?" The limp cotton dresses moved closer. Maybelle hunched over them and said: "Louise Finley's gonna have a baby, and I know who the daddy is!"

The girls shrieked and Maybelle was rewarded. Her round arms squashed down all who-told-yous and where'd-you-hear-thats. "Furthermore," she said, "Louise's being sent to a home in Mobile for unwed mothers tomorrow. 'Course her daddy sent the sheriff after the Eddards boy—he's the one done it. Way Mr. Finley found out was Louise told Dr. Simmons about it, and he told him and my daddy and I heard Daddy tellin' Mamma. Mamma liked to broke a blood-vessel and said the Christian shame of it, those Finleys ought to be destroyed by the State, an' said it was that

Mr. Finley's fault because he let that girl run wild all over the place, an' said Mr. Finley'd never be able to hold up his head again!" Maybelle licked her lips. "Tell you one thing," she said slowly, "that Mildred and Louise Finley'd better not show their faces in the Mexia community any more. It's a disgrace to this county, that's what it is!"

Abbie felt sick. "Louise's only about your age, isn't she?"

"Yeah. Few months younger, I guess."

When Abbie was puzzled her eyes opened wide and she rubbed the back of her head. "But Louise can't be having a baby. She's not even married, Maybelle."

Maybelle grinned at the girls. "Oh yes she can, stupid." Taking a deep breath, she added softly: "Listen, honey, you can have a baby any time after you're twelve. Hell, I coulda had one at eleven. . . . You have a man against you and—Abbie, ain't you started yet?"

"Yes. Last month."

"Well, then you oughta know about it."

"What do you mean, Maybelle? Know about what?" Abbie's sweaty hands twisted her dress hem into a dirty wad. Her stomach churned and a dull heaviness crept into her shoulders. Maybelle's blonde plaits seemed to stand out sharply against the sky, the high-school building behind her shifted a little.

"All right," the plaits wagged, "get this and get it straight: If a man touches you after you've started you'll have a solid baby!" Maybelle smacked her palm on the bench.

The color left Abbie's face, and she heard her own voice come from inside the high-school building. "You mean if a boy asks you to—?"

"That's right. And if you do it you'll have a baby," the plaits nodded triumphantly. "That Louise Finley—hey, what's the matter Ab?"

She awoke, feeling a soggy cloth against her face and Miss Nash's halitosis on her eyelids. Abbie felt herself being pulled from the ground. "I'm going to send you home for the balance of the day," said Miss Nash. The record clicked back into place: "Can you get home all right by yourself?"

"Yessum." Abbie lived around the corner from the school, only a short walk.

"Tell your mother you got a little too hot out here," Miss Nash's stiff white false teeth grinned at her.

Arms on hips, Mrs. Henderson waited until Abbie climbed the steps and entered the cool dusky hallway. "Have you been fighting again?" she asked. "Miss Nash called and said you were on the way home, and you'd tell me about it." Mrs. Henderson pushed her down the hall.

"I fainted, Mamma."

Her mother's frown faded. "Oh. I'd better get you something. Go lie down."

She spit most of the milky ammonia-and-water back into the glass, turned on her stomach and lay silently until Mrs. Henderson left the room.

As the door creaked shut Abbie closed her eyes. She trembled violently under the sheet; a tight mass worked its way up her windpipe, and she opened her mouth to let it out. *Oh, God*, she prayed, *don't let me—don't let me! I'll do anything if you won't let me—!* The heaviness in her shoulders crept slowly down her arms; her knees and thighs ached. *Please, God, I want to die. I didn't mean to. I didn't know—*. Oh God. They would send her away to Mobile and she'd never see them again. There was that Ames girl once. . . . The Ameses left Maiben County and never came back. . . . Everybody in the county knew the Hendersons; they would have to go away over to Barbour—no, Uncle Dick lived there. What would they do without her? She saw her father walking home from work, looking down the street for Abbie to run meet him and seeing nothing but Brantley's Store. He went in the house and took off his straw hat. Mother, he said. In the kitchen, Jim, she said. When Mr. Henderson touched her, she cried. They sat alone in the livingroom night after night wondering what had happened to Abbie in Mobile. . . .

Abbie groaned and let out another lump. Every dirty word she knew sang in her brain—what did they really mean? There it was: she was going to have a baby, all right. O God, what would her mother and father say?

What of Ed Dennis? He didn't mean to, he wouldn't if he had known. Until today, she had forgotten Ed Dennis with his pants unbuttoned hugging her, so long ago. No, it was last Tuesday afternoon. They had been playing kickball in the backyard and, tired, had dropped to the ground behind the carhouse. "Abbie," he had said. "Let me see you. I just want to see what a girl looks like."

Now if they found out the sheriff would put him in the ratty town jail, because of her. Poor Ed, nothing wrong with him. They had known each other since they were born, and that time Ed sliced his leg halfway up Abbie took him a get-well present. She thought of everything about Ed Dennis: his father ran the Cas-A-Loma filling station on the edge of town and had two fingers missing; his mother was a Nazarene; he had two grown sisters. . . .

She jerked on her back and stared at the knotholes in the blue wooden ceiling. Count the cracks, she thought, like that time you had scarlet fever. Count the cracks and they'll turn into days, the baby will come and you'll be caught. . . . Mrs. Dee Peavy across the street will run over to tell Mrs. Burkett about the shame of those Hendersons and they'll look at your daddy when he walks home from the office. . . . Suddenly she giggled and sat up straight.

She kicked the sheet off and got up: why, it wouldn't happen for a week at least and when it did she'd hide it under the house by the chimney! "Mamma," she called. "I'm feeling better now, can I get up?"

"No, you stay right there a while longer," said Mrs. Henderson's voice from deep in the kitchen.

She lay back on the bed. The tension crawled out through her fingertips, leaving her tired. Soon she slept.

But her assurance was short-lived. At school, daily discussions with Group Two affirmed that: if somebody had a baby who wasn't supposed to they'd be sent by law to a home, and their father would lose his business. He couldn't get a job wherever he went because what happened would always follow him. Babies? Oh, they grew inside your stomach and were born when you went to the bathroom. It hurt a lot. Yeah, any boy over twelve could give you one.

Her father swore he didn't know what was the matter with that child. Why in a week's time she had turned sulky;

when she wasn't moping around she was sitting back of the carhouse. When he called her name she looked up like she expected him to hit her.

"Oh, you know what it is, Jim," Mrs. Henderson said. "She hasn't been started long and's not used to it yet."

"But you explained everything, didn't you?" Jim Henderson thought he knew girls, but he'd never seen one take it like Abbie.

"I thought I did," said her mother.

When it happened, her first reaction was disbelief, then horror. Her mother had put her on the bed and told her she would have it every month. Abbie was too frightened to ask many questions, and her mother did no more than answer them. Jim Henderson chuckled when he remembered how Abbie had come to him for confirmation. He'd had the hardest time persuading her that it was natural, that all girls had it, that she would not have to stop playing ball but just take it easier from now on. "After all, Abbie, you're growing up."

She had screamed, "I don't want to grow up if this is what happens all the time!" and had run outdoors. That evening at suppertime Jim Henderson found her crouched behind the carhouse, close against the wall. It had been a task to make her come in.

To make matters worse, everybody at school had known

why she was absent a day: when she would not play town-ball at recess, Ed Dennis grinned and told Raymond Walters something. Raymond laughed and looked toward Abbie.

Now, each day she sat in the schoolroom looking vaguely at some orange cut-outs some long-gone sixth grade had pasted on the blackboard. Her skirt was always streaked with dirt where she had rubbed it, her palms would not stop sweating.

In the purgatory between wakefulness and sleep she found peace, but when she was fully roused it came back and stared at her. Sometimes during the day when there was an interesting history period or a close ballgame, she forgot for a while. Every Saturday afternoon when she was Hoot Gibson she forgot, but it flashed on the screen when the last shots faded away. Maybelle had said there was a doctor in the county who laid you on a kitchen table and cut you open for fifty dollars, but who had fifty dollars? She remembered the Sunday Mr. Q W Tatum preached on Girls for Sale and how he had said: "Mothers, warn your daughters! Daughters, obey your mothers!"

Abbie looked for the baby every morning when she got up, and prayed it would come out when she mashed her abdomen. She rapidly accumulated more information from Group Two; sometimes there would be heartening news:

your stomach swelled and you got sick sometimes. Abbie's stomach was so flat the hipbones stuck out. Aside from a no-feeling always near her ribs she felt fine. Sometimes you went to a hospital and had it cut out, but only rich people could afford it. It took nine or ten months for a baby to come, sometimes a year: this was the most encouraging thing yet—she had time.

So far as she knew, neither her mother nor her father suspected anything. She could see the dreadful look on her father's face if she told him—maybe he would lock her in the carhouse and let her die, and tell the sheriff she got lost and wasn't found until three days later. Maybe he would smother her with a pillow—no, he wouldn't. He'd send her away.

"Daddy," she said one afternoon as she collected her daily ice-cream nickel. "What's killing a baby called?" She looked at the Code of Alabama on the office shelves.

"Murder." Jim Henderson put down a paper and stared at Abbie.

"You go to the pen for it, don't you?"

"Of course, if you don't get electrocuted." A line appeared between his thick black brows. "You know that, Abbie. Killing a child is like killing a grown man."

"Yessir. I was just thinking about something . . ."

"You look like you've been thinking peculiar things

lately, Abbie," he said. Might as well let her know now. "What's the matter with you? You've been moping around for weeks, now. You won't eat, you look like a scarecrow, you're nasty to your mother and won't do a thing she tells you. If you aren't careful you're going to get a dose of oil and my belt on your bottom." The paper snapped as he picked it up. Queerest child he'd ever seen.

"Yessir." Abbie looked at the floor.

"Well, run along now. I'm busy."

She walked across the small green square to Dr. Simmons's office. She stood in the doorway, swinging the screen back and forth. "Hi, Uncle Charlie!" she said.

Dr. Simmons swung around. "You're just in time to watch the office, Abbie. Miss Metts and I have a call."

Abbie ran a finger over her nose. "Be gone long?"

"Can't tell. If we aren't back by five, just snap the lock on the door." Dr. Simmons probed his pocket, found a quarter and thumped it on the desk. "Bye. Don't fool with anything, now."

When Dr. Simmons and his nurse were in the car, Abbie jumped from the wicker chair. She loved to explore the drawers of white bandages, finger glistening instruments and tubes in the glass cabinet, but this afternoon she pulled down a red leather book called *Diseases of Women* and began turning the pages. Pictures of swollen women draped in white sheets, things that looked like ice tongs, long slender knives and open, bleeding wounds leaped up at her. She threw the book down, ran to the back door and hung her head over the steps. She wiped her mouth, then ran all the way home and sat behind the garage until dark.

The idea came to her one afternoon when Mrs. Henderson sent her to the ice-house. As Abbie pulled her wagon down the road she glanced up at the town water tank, the tallest thing in Maiben County. She frowned a moment, then felt her stomach. They said you could hear its heart beat—her own pulse pounded beneath her hand. It was there, no use denying it. Nothing would take it away: she had tried beating on her stomach so many times, but it wouldn't come until it got good and ready. Maybelle said you could tell when one started to come, and there wouldn't be one if. . . .

She looked carefully at the tank, pink and silver in the late afternoon sun: Maiben Water Service Company, it said, and swayed in the sky. She pulled her wagon up to its base and leaped to the tank ladder's bottom rung. She grasped the thin steel sides and climbed quickly; there would be red marks on her feet if she did not hurry, the rungs were hot. Halfway up she looked down: the ground moved. She looked up: the tank still swayed. Abbie closed her eyes and climbed until her head bumped against the platform railing.

All the town was beneath her: the white courthouse dome rose above tired oaks; the tar roof on her uncle's office was buckling and cracking in the heat; store buildings with their tin roofs clustered around the square. There was her house to the left, the chinaberry trees in a sandy backyard, the old carhouse and beside it her playhouse. She thought she could make out Mr. Ben Watts walking down the street, but was not sure.

Maybelle said your stomach would hurt before it came, she thought. When it does I'll have time to get here, maybe. They'll miss me, but I can't bear to go to Mobile. She giggled: the tears in her eyes made the square look crazy and shaky, so she wiped her eyes. A bug flying at full speed splattered against her cheek. She said, "Hell," and wiped the green remains on her sleeve.

The Methodist church would be full for her funeral, the Hendersons knew everybody. Smilax would cover the choir-loft to hide Miss Eva Kilpatrick and the organ from the congregation, and Mr. Q W Tatum would preach in low wails. Quietly the family would file by the open casket to see her for the last time, and a nod from her father would close the casket lid. Her cousins would carry her from the church, the honorary pallbearers would pick up the flowers, the congregation would rise and file out, but they would always remember

Abbie Catherine Henderson

Born 1926 Died 1938

Jesus Loved Her.

Are you dead when you're falling or do you die when you hit the ground?

When you hit the ground, surely. The green-and-yellow stubble below looked soft, like a patchwork quilt on the ground. Funny, how grass grows in circles around sandbeds.

The sky was darkening as she descended. She heard only her heavy breathing and the soft thud of her bare feet on each rung. When she reached the ground she hopped a moment on each foot to make the ground-shock leave her toes and legs.

Abbie smiled as she started for home. It would give her a warning when it wanted to come, Maybelle said they did, and she'd have time—. She picked up some flat rocks and skipped one along the ground. She saw a brown dog and flung one at him. She laughed when he yelped, then sighed deeply. After all, you don't have to think of anything while you're falling.

The

BINOCULARS

MY BROTHER WAS SIX YEARS older than I, a slender boy with brown hair which he did not begin slicking back with water until he was fifteen. Each evening my jealousy of him reached its peak when, at the supper table or in the living-room before bedtime, he would relate what had happened at school that morning, never failing to draw Miss Busey and Miss Maxwell, two of the grammar-school teachers, into the story.

I had never met either of the ladies: Miss Busey lived on the Ridge, Miss Maxwell stayed with her mother in Mexia, Alabama. Both rode the school bus into town each morning: Mexia and the Ridge were about ten miles from Maiben, the county seat and site of the county grammar school.

For almost a year I had watched them every school day through our back fence. Our house was around the corner from the school, close enough for us to hear the "taking-in," recess, and dinner bells. Through the fence palings I could see short red and brown and yellow shapes playing during recess and noon on the hard clay of the schoolyard. Occasionally, two dark women came out of the door together and strolled on the concrete sidewalk in front of the school building. Apparently they were overseeing the children;

sometimes one of the women would raise an arm, a child would leave the group and run over to them. They would stand together for a moment, then the child would resume its play.

For Christmas I demanded and received a pair of toy black binoculars from my grown sister who lived in Birmingham. They were powerful enough to bring the faces in the schoolyard close to me, and most of the time I kept the binoculars trained on the front door, hoping that Miss Busey and Miss Maxwell would appear in the two merging circles of light. Edwin, my brother, said that I would have Miss Maxwell for the first grade, but would have to wait until I was in the fifth for Miss Busey. Miss Busey had been his teacher last year. “She’s not so hot, Dody,” he said. “Wait’ll you get in the seventh. They have a homeroom teacher and switch classrooms every period.”

The thought of waiting so long for Miss Busey was not painful when I considered the long drowsy year in Miss Maxwell’s room. Once, while looking through the binoculars, I saw Miss Maxwell glance around the schoolyard, then take a compact and an orange tube from her black purse. It must have been Tangee lipstick; it was the same kind of tube I found in an old box my sister had left in the front-room bureau drawer. Miss Maxwell held the compact in front of her face and put the tube to her mouth. When it came away she pressed her lips together firmly. They were soft and pink.

Miss Busey wore two yellow pencils in her brown hair, which was done up in piles on top of her head. My brother said the pencils held her hair up. “One day she forgot and pulled one out and her hair came down,” he said. She was thin, and her dresses always seemed to fit too loosely. Miss Maxwell was not quite so tall. If Miss Busey had worn her hair in bangs, they would have been about the same height.

Before my sister sent the binoculars, Miss Maxwell and Miss Busey were only dark shapes getting off the bus together in the mornings, walking slowly up and down the sidewalk often alone but sometimes together, hurrying toward the outdoor toilet—Miss Maxwell went at ten every morning and smoked, I could see blue wisps drifting up from the privy ventilator; Miss Busey waited until noon. I was perhaps the only person in town who knew Miss Maxwell smoked, but I promised myself never to give away her secret, she could depend on me not to tell anyone. Perhaps when I entered the first grade she would allow me to stay after school and clean the blackboards, something my brother said she forced him to do when he was in her room. Then maybe she would take out a cigarette and wink at me. “Bet you didn’t know I smoked. There’s nobody here but you and me, so this is just between us, you know," she would say.

A long summer passed, September 17, 1932, came, and I was finally old enough to enter the first grade. Miss Maxwell would not have to introduce herself to me, I would go up and tell her I knew her already. I would say that I'd seen her occasionally in the schoolyard, and that my brother had told me all about her because she was his favorite teacher, a flat lie.

My mother thought I could go alone to school the first day. She gave me two satsumas from the dining-room safe, a nickel for milk to wash down the satsumas, and my vaccination certificate.

In the first-grade room were four rows of maroon desks, a Franklin stove, and two rag-streaked blackboards. The five windows on one side of the room were decorated with orange cutouts of witches and pumpkins. Little smears of dried paste streaked the cutouts and the glass around them. Under the windows was a long shelf half filled with thin dingy blue books. A large rectangular desk was in front of the blackboard, and behind it sat a thin woman with a wide fleshy nose and black greying hair. The skin on her cheekbones was orange, almost matching the cutouts. She seemed to know me: she motioned for me to come to the desk. I put my vaccination certificate on top of a stack of white envelopes. "We haven't begun yet," she said. "Run out and play until the bell rings."

"Who are you?" I asked.

"I am Miss Turnipseed," she said, and laughed. "You'll have a lot of fun out of my name this year."

"Where is Miss Maxwell? Isn't she going to be here?"

"No. Miss Maxwell got married last summer. I'm your teacher this year," said Miss Turnipseed. "I've got a funny name, and don't mind one bit if you laugh at it."

"Yessum," I said. "Is Miss Busey still here? She teaches the fifth grade, I think."

"No. Margaret—Miss Busey, I mean, has gone to Livingstone for her M.A. Didn't you know that teachers have to go to school, too?"

From somewhere in the hall a bell rang, and the low hum from the schoolyard spattered into sentences as children came into the room. My friends—Anne Hines, Sara Ann McCall, Percy Dunnam, John Jr. Hybart, Rayford Smith—ran to desks by the windows. "Save me one!" I called.

The inside of the desk was empty and dusty; my palm was brown where I had rubbed it across the splintery pine wood. I put my satsumas in the desk, and looked around. The town children sat together. As I had not been among the first to grab a seat, I was on the outer edges: across the aisle were strange children dressed in faded cotton prints and denim shirts buttoned all the way up. Their hair was stuck down with water; the girls wore thick black bobby pins.

Directly behind me sat Eddie May Ousley, a girl who lived on the edge of town and tried to run around with us, but we snubbed her and talked in whispers whenever she came near. She was a year older than most of us and a "failure"—in 1932 failures were not allowed special privileges, they were treated like beginners. I resented her sitting behind me, but thought that her experience might prove useful.

I grinned at her and said, "Hey, Eddie May."

For no particular reason she giggled and stuck her fingers down the back of my dress collar. I yelped in surprise, and Miss Turnipseed heard me.

"What is the matter?" she asked.

"Nothing. Eddie May just stuck her cold hands down my back," I said.

Miss Turnipseed frowned. "Eddie May Ousley," she said loudly. "Just go over and take your place in the corner. I will not have a disturbance out of you on the first day!"

"But Miss—." I tried to help her, but it was no use. Eddie May had a corner by the window, though, and Sara Ann and Percy Dunnam said it wasn't my fault.

When Miss Turnipseed tapped a pencil on her desk the

class subsided into a nervous silence. “We won’t do much today,” she smiled. “We’ll divide into groups. Group One,” she pointed to Anne Hines, “will be from Anne on back. Group Two is the balance of the room.” She had neatly divided the class into town children and bus children.

When Group One was called to the blackboard, I found a place by Percy. “What’s this for?” he asked, lisping slightly.

“I don’t know,” I said aloud.

“Shh!” Miss Turnipseed put a finger to her lips. She went down the line of children and handed each a long piece of fresh chalk. She then wrote each child’s name in large round script on the board in front of him.

“Now trace your names,” she said.

I wrote mine underneath Miss Turnipseed’s effort and returned to my desk. When she saw what I had done Miss Turnipseed said, “Come here.” Chalk was sighing and squeaking against the board as she led me to it. “There’s no point in trying to show everybody how smart you are. I told you to *trace* your name.”

My palms began to sweat. “Yessum,” I said. “I’m sorry, I didn’t mean to—.”

“Now trace,” she said.

I picked up some chalk and moved it over the last o of my surname. “Not that way,” she said harshly, and pressed her finger on the beginning of the first N. When she took it away there was a black greasy mark. "You start here. Haven't you ever traced anything before?"

"Nome."

"Hasn't your mother ever let you trace pictures out of a magazine?"

"Nome," I said. "Mamma lets me draw, though."

Miss Turnipseed looked at me sharply. "Where did you learn to write?"

"Mamma taught me," I said. "A long time ago."

Miss Turnipseed's throat twitched. "Can you read, too?"

"Yessum, but I can't—."

She sat down at her desk and pulled a blue sheet of paper out of the middle drawer. "Your mother's not supposed to do that. Tell her she's not supposed to do that. She's not supposed to teach you to read. You're not supposed to be able to read and write when you first come to school!" She looked angrily at the paper, picked up a fountain pen and began writing.

"Take this to your mother when you go home," she said, folding the paper once and holding it out toward me. "And don't read it on the way," she sneered.

Miss Maxwell and Miss Busey would have known I couldn't help it.

The

PINKING SHEARS

AFTER IT WAS ALL OVER Daddy said it was my fault, but to this day I say it isn't, that the child had a perfect right to cut her own hair if she wanted to. Well, I sort of cut it, but Matrid told me to. How would I know it was against the laws of God? There is nothing in the *Discipline Of The Methodist Episcopal Church, South* that says it's sinful to cut your hair, and if Mr. Q W Tatum says it is from the pulpit he's the one that's wrong, not me.

You'll notice I didn't put any periods after the Q and W in Mr. Tatum's name. That's not my fault either. When Mr. Q W came to Hatter's Mill, Alabama, in a high square 1929 Buick with nine children in it, Mr. Ed at the *Journal* office put this notice in the paper:

> We are pleased to publish the fact that Mr. and Mrs. Q. W. Tatum and their children, Haniel, Job, Habbakuk, Matrid, Jezebel, Mary, Hosea and Hosannah (twins) and Emmanuel Tatum have arrived from the Methodist Church in Dothan. Mr. Tatum will fill the pulpit of the Hatter's Mill Methodist Church for the next four years.

Well, the first thing Mr. Q W did when he got his children and belongings into the parsonage was to go down to the *Journal* office and tell Mr. Ed to never again put periods after Q W, that Q W was his *name*, not his initials. And furthermore, Habakkuk was spelled wrong, so watch that in the future. Mr. Ed got right upset at it and called Daddy, who was chairman of the Board of Stewards and whose business it was to look after the new preacher. Daddy said please be careful about it because he had had a time getting that preacher here all the way from Dothan, and to be sure to come over to the pounding they were having for him Wednesday night.

It was at the pounding that I first met Matrid. When Daddy and I started up the parsonage steps that night with our groceries, somebody reached out from under the porch and took hold of Daddy's ankle. My father's an awkward man, so he fell and scattered his pound of Irish potatoes all over the yard. About that time a great black-headed man came rushing out of the house hollering, "How're you, Brother Finch, welcome! And this is little Jean Louie. Have you been baptized with that wonderful spirit yet?"

He scared me to death so all I could do was say, "Yes sir, when I was nine months old."

Mr. Q W helped Daddy to his feet and then bent double

under the steps. For a few minutes we heard an awful muffle and scuffle, then he came out dragging the dirtiest child I ever saw by the longest hair I ever saw on any one human. Mr. Q W stood her up and slapped her face with one hand and her behind with the other. She just stood there taking it: if it had been me you could have heard me yelling to hell and back.

When he finally finished Mr. Q W said, "Now march in that house and read three chapters of Jeremiah, you terrible child!"

She turned to go but he caught her shoulder. "Wait! Can't you remember your manners? Matrid, this is Brother Finch and Miss Jean Louie Finch. You and Jean Louie are in the same class at school."

Matrid looked up at Daddy, and Daddy smiled at her like Jesus and patted that mess of tangled hair on her head.

"What grade you in?" she scowled at me.

"Third," I said.

"Can you read good?"

"Yeah, I'm in the first group." This seemed to make an impression because her eyes widened and she grinned at me fit to kill.

"I can't read," she said.

I used to be right sniffy at people who couldn't read but I

didn't have any business being that way. I've since learned that people can be smart in other various ways without knowing how to read. Matrid, I found out later, was one of them.

We went inside, and there in the living room was lined up the funniest bunch of folks you ever saw: all the boys (five of 'em) had thick black hair that looked like it had been cut with a pair of hedge-clippers. They all had on denim shirts buttoned clear up to the collar and no ties. The girls were even worse, being attired in the same stuff you make flour sacks out of. Each one had on long sleeves though it was a boiling night.

Mrs. Tatum, who stood at the end of the line, was a tub of a woman with red cheeks and hands. She never said anything the whole night.

As more and more folks came into the parsonage bringing their gifts, the children showed signs of getting tired. But let me tell you those people stood in that line two hours until Mr. Q W all of a sudden snapped, "Fall out!"

This sounded like sheer regimentation to me, so I turned to Matrid, who had stuck to me like a wood-tick instead of reading Jeremiah like she was supposed to.

"What do you do around this place?" I asked. "It's got only one bathroom."

"Oh," she said. "When we have to get up to go to school we start at six in the morning. The oldest of us gets the bathroom first. I wash Haniel's back and he sees that the twins move their bowels. It works real well—the old ones kind of look after the young ones."

"I reckon you have to in a family this large."

"Yeah, Mamma and Daddy have enough to do as it is, with Daddy circuit preaching and Mamma doing all his visiting for him."

She looked at me like she thought I had a wart on my head and said, "Come on in the back room and I'll show you my water."

I didn't quite know what to make of this. Matrid took me by the hand and led me down the dark narrow hall. She opened a door and we went into a room that was filled with cots one on top of another, bunk fashion.

"Here's where we sleep," she said.

She went into the closet and came out carrying a cardboard box with writing on it. Laying it carefully on the floor in the middle of the room, she fumbled with the dirty cord a while, couldn't untie it, and slid it over the side. I then smelled the stinkingest odor I ever smelled in my life.

In the box was a lot of bottles, big ones and little ones, full of water. Matrid picked up one with some dark brown stuff in it and said, "This is the most precious one I have. It came from the River Avon."

"Where's that?" I asked.

"It's in England, stupid. Way across the Atlantic Ocean. I'm going there some day because they have a lot of heathens. Daddy says they don't like Methodists over there so when I get big I'm going over as a missionary."

She sat down on the bed, her hair streaming down her face like a crazy woman's. I couldn't take my eyes off it.

"Show me some more," I said.

Matrid pulled out bottle after bottle, telling me where the water in each one came from. She had samples from all over the state of Alabama, including some of that artesian stuff from Hatter's Mill that our town is named after. I was so taken up with Matrid's water collection I almost forgot she didn't know how to read. That girl was smart! She knew everything about foreign places!

But I couldn't keep my eyes off the hair. It looked like it hadn't been combed in a month, and it all fell over her face so she had a hard time seeing through it.

"Matrid," I said. "Why do you let your hair go like that?"

She looked down in her lap and didn't say anything for a while. Then she squatted on the floor and began putting her bottles back in the box.

"I hate my hair," she said softly. "Mamma won't let me cut it. I'm the only one in my family with long hair. Daddy cuts Haniel and them's once every two weeks but he won't cut mine. I've never had a haircut."

She looked at my bangs and said, "How does it feel to have short hair?"

"Oh, all right, I guess. Real easy to comb. I just give it a couple of swats in the morning and it stays this way all day."

I reckon I said the wrong thing because Matrid started crying like she'd never quit. She did, though, and started picking her nose.

"Why won't your Mamma let you cut it?" I asked, real casually. I didn't want to appear too curious but was just dying to know.

"Well," she sniffed. "I'm the first girl and Mamma said she was always going to make the first girl have long hair, because her sister that died had hair so long you could sit down on it."

"What's that got to do with it?" It all sounded right strange to me.

"You see, Auntie was real bad and men used to come for miles around to see her with her long hair. She would use it to make herself pretty to 'em with."

I thought Matrid was going to poke her finger clear up

to her brains so I told her if she didn't stop I'd hit her. She snuffed it up and went on talking.

"My aunt was awful, Mamma said, and we couldn't have much to do with her. But she was always real nice to me. Auntie said I looked like her and used to bring me bracelets, but Daddy never would let me wear 'em. Finally one day she got sick and said she had to go down to Mobile. She went and never did come back. Daddy went after her and found that she had died."

"But what's that got to do with you?"

"Mamma talks to me for an hour once a week about being a good girl and never to be sinful like Auntie was, and to let my hair grow long to take Auntie's place and be good."

"Well hell," I said. "If you don't like it—"

"Shut your mouth, Jean Louie!" said Matrid. "If you keep on talking like that I'll have to stop up my ears. That's bad talk! If you talk like that you're going there."

"O.K., O.K., I won't say it any more! But Matrid, I don't see why you can't be just as good with your hair short as with it long. Why, look at me! Mine's short and I go to Sunday School and Church and the League. I'm just as good as you are—maybe better than you."

"That's not for you to say," said Matrid in a prissy voice.

She went to the drawer and looked in the mirror, pulling her fingers roughly through her hair.

Lord, that child looked sorrowful. She started crying again, her tears running down the limp strings of her hair and dropping off on the floor.

That did it. I don't know what made me do it, but all I knew then was that Matrid hated her hair long. I couldn't stand to think of her having to go through life with that briar-patch on her head. Even if she couldn't read she knew a lot of things I didn't.

"Got any scissors?" I asked.

"Yeah." She opened the dresser drawer and pulled out a pair of pinking shears. "This is what Mamma uses to cut cloth with. I don't know whether they'll cut anything else. What do you want with 'em, Jean Louie?"

"Never you mind," I said. "You just come over here and sit on the bed and I'll show you."

Matrid slumped on the bed and looked up at me. "What're you going to do?"

"Cut it off."

She didn't say a word—just sat there like she was a Confederate tombstone. I grabbed a wad of hair and whacked. The shears snicked off a hunk about a foot long, with nice little scalloped edges. That child must have had a ton of hair, because when I got it all off on the floor it was up to Matrid's ankles.

"Now go look at yourself," said I. It really did look good, only kind of chewed. But it was short like mine.

Watching herself in the mirror, Matrid giggled. She hopped up and down and did a little dance around the beds.

"Gee, I feel a hundred pounds lighter, Jean Louie. I won't have to rassle with it any more. It was just plain torture for me to have to comb it."

"Well, it won't be any more," I said. It did me proud to see Matrid so happy. She looked different, too. Her face sort of came out—her cheeks were rounder and you could see her forehead.

Just then the door opened and Daddy poked his head around it. "Jean Louie! Time to go, honey," he said. Then he saw the pile of hair on the floor.

"What's that?"

"Matrid's hair," I said.

"I see, you all have been playing Beauty Shop. Well, you'd better clean it up before we go."

Daddy heard Mr. Q W's voice in the back hall and stepped aside to let him come in.

"Look," Daddy said, laughing. "Have you ever seen such a mess?"

Mr. Q W came in and froze. His eyes bulged out and he got redder in the face every second. He said to me in a choky voice, "What have you done to my child? What have you done to her?"

He grabbed me by the shoulders and started shaking me until I thought my head would fall off. I yelled and jerked free, running to hide behind Daddy. I held on to Daddy's overcoat for dear life and screamed at him not to let Mr. Q W get me. Daddy whispered to be quiet, nothing was going to happen.

Mr. Q W was down on the floor picking up handfuls of Matrid's hair. He stood up and made motions like he was trying to put it back on her head again. Mr. Q W discovered this was impossible because he turned to my father and gasped, "Oh that heathen child! Brother Finch, take Jean Louie home and make her get on her knees and ask the Lord to forgive her for what she's done! Make her pray all night long. You'll never understand what she's done—oh my God, my God forgive her!"

Daddy just stood there and didn't say anything, but he got that squint-eyed look I know so well when he's losing his temper.

Finally in a voice like a graveyard he said, "Brother Tatum, I don't know what Jean Louie's done that's so terrible. In fact, I can't see that she's done anything but cut Matrid's hair, which I must say needed cutting. If you care to explain the circumstances to me, pointing out the sin in Jean Louie's actions, I shall see that the proper corrective measures are taken."

I thought that was a right nice speech, but Daddy's a lawyer and can talk good anyway.

Except it had a chaotic effect on Mr. Q W: the man literally had a hissy there in the middle of the floor. He stomped and shouted texts from the Bible: "My sins are in number as the hairs on my head" being the most frequently used. He also said something about Matrid's aunt being a bad woman in Mobile and that Matrid was going to take her place in the world. Mr. Q W acted more like a Holy Roller than a Methodist preacher, so we just stood there taking it all in.

Daddy finally called him down, only after Mr. Q W said he'd preach a sermon on it in church next Sunday and make me stand up and apologize for what I'd done right in the middle of the congregation.

Daddy said we had to go home, and that Jean Louie wouldn't stand up and apologize for anything.

"Say good-bye to Matrid," he said. "And ask her to come to see you."

I looked over at Matrid, who had hidden her face in a pillow. "Come to see me," I said. "I'm sorry I cut off your hair."

As we walked down the sidewalk toward home that night, Daddy didn't say anything. He just went along looking straight in front of him, not saying a word, which is a good sign I've done something wrong.

Presently he horked and spit on the pavement and cleared his throat for a long time. He said, "It was your fault, baby. You shouldn't have done it."

"Yessir, I guess so," said I, having that no-feeling in the pit of my stomach. "Will I have to ask Matrid to forgive me in church?"

Daddy took my hand and swung it up with his. He didn't answer for a long time, so I passed it by blowing my breath into the chilly night air and pretending I was smoking cigarettes.

"Jean Louie," he said finally. "When you get grown and go to the Law School you'll learn that you have to weigh the evidence and decide which party has been injured the most."

He looked down at me. "Do you understand what I'm saying?"

I said, "Sure," but I didn't. I did know that everything was all right, though, by the tone of his voice.

"Well," he continued slowly. "This time it was a matter of who was the most to blame—you or Matrid's father. Do you see what I mean?"

I nodded as hard as I could.

We reached the front door of our house, and as Daddy was opening it I said, "Are you sure I won't have to stand up in church and apologize to Matrid?"

Daddy shook his head. "No, you won't have to do that—Mr. Tatum won't ask you to." He jerked the door open and grinned. "But let's be sure and go to church Sunday to see just what he says!"

A

ROOMFUL *of* KIBBLE

MY FRIEND SARAH MITCHELL IS having a hard time living with herself these days, and I shouldn't wonder, after what she did. She's made every excuse under the sun for it, and has worn her poor old psychiatrist to a nub trying to find new ones. It was I who suggested to Sarah that she go to a psychiatrist, hoping Sarah would call *him* at all hours instead of me. The other day I had a talk with her psychiatrist, who is not a man but an elderly lady, and she told me what Sarah's trouble was, but it sounded completely unreal to me. Poor old lady, she also complained that she was damn tired of having Sarah call at three in the morning to tell her somebody was banging on the apartment door, a surprisingly human complaint considering the source.

Even before it happened, Sarah was something of a problem, no doubt about it. I've known her for years—we were at the University together, and even then she was something of a curiosity: she would get drunk on about two drinks, pass out stiff on the floor, and nothing, not even threats of expulsion, could get her off it. Many's the night I've jumped in her bed to cover up for her when the housemother would come around checking to see who was and who wasn't there, and Sarah would be out cold in somebody's apartment. She wouldn't remember a thing the next day.

And another thing, she was a compulsive curser. I have never come across anyone with a finer command of language than Sarah Mitchell, nor anyone who used it more impartially: deans, beaus, waitresses, postal authorities, anybody who came within range if Sarah happened to be on a cursing jag. This habit earned her the eternal suspicion of the Dean of Women's office, the denizens of which were just waiting for an excuse to ship her. In the due course of events, they did, for having a bottle of beer in her possession. That doesn't sound so terrible, but it is when you learn it's the University of Alabama I refer to. There, young ladies are expected to smell of nothing more than Chanel No. 5 and Lavoris for at least four years.

Anyway, Sarah left the University under a thundercloud. Suspected: cheating, stealing, sneaking out of Calloway Hall at night, promiscuity, and an irreverent attitude toward the Dean of Women. Proven: one bottle of beer in her hand. Of course, she didn't have to parade down University Avenue with it—that was rather indiscreet—but they shipped her for it.

When she was packing to leave, Sarah was in a fury, the main point of her discourse being that that mealy-mouthed

Georgine Faircloth only got six weeks' strict campus for being caught buck naked in a rowboat on the Black Warrior River, and here, she, Sarah Mitchell, was being expelled because her father hadn't had his money as long as Georgine's had had his. Besides, Georgine was a Beta Nu, and everybody who so much as pledged Beta Nu was assured of a free pass through the University, since the sorority was founded by Mrs. Jefferson Davis's sister. Sarah had been rushed by the Beta Nus and was dropped like a hot brick the first time she opened her mouth, but if it hurt her nobody knew it. She just set about becoming the most independent independent on the campus.

In her second year she got secretly married, which was worse than drinking, and divorced, which was worse than getting married. He was an awfully peculiar boy from Birmingham who thought he was better than everybody else in general and Sarah in particular. Sarah's father got her out of that one and never let her hear the last of how much it cost him. Mr. Mitchell was a rich man, but five dollars was a lot of money to him, because long ago he had been a poor man. Sarah's mother was a gilt-edged horror. She was one of those women who laugh and say heehoo on the end of it, which passes for gentility in some parts of the state. Without actually saying anything, Mrs. Mitchell always managed to convey the impression that even the time of day was improper; she long ago admitted to herself that Sarah was her shame, the price she had paid for isolated acts of impropriety with her husband, and she treated Sarah accordingly.

No wonder Sarah headed straight for New York when she left school. Her parents wouldn't have her home anyway; they enjoyed their martyrdom far too much to have it destroyed by her presence: people in her home town were terribly nice to the Mitchells when it got out that Sarah had been shipped, and in two weeks they received more supper invitations than they had in a year.

I hadn't heard of or from Sarah Mitchell until two years later when I went to live in New York and ran into her on Fifth Avenue. You know how that is, sooner or later you meet everybody you ever knew on Fifth Avenue. Well, there she was. She greeted me with the usual questions and asked me if I would go home with her and see her boys. "Boys?" I said. "I didn't know you were married again."

"I'm not," she said. Same old Sarah.

But there was something different about her I couldn't figure out at first. Something physical. She'd put on weight, of course, as we all do two years out of college, and she looked tidier than I'd ever seen her, but with that coat on you really couldn't tell. Finally I got it: her hands. She had big square hands, cotton-picking hands, she used to call them, but her fingers were long and they went out at the ends instead of tapering off. For the first time since I'd known her I became aware of how awkwardly she used them; she seemed to have trouble with the most ordinary things, like reaching into her pocketbook for bus fare. She kept her fingers straight when it would be natural to bend them. From time to time she would rub the heel of one hand down the side of her coat as though to remove perspiration, although the day was cold. In all other respects, Sarah was her old self.

When we got to her apartment I met the boys. They were two huge dogs I took to be mastiffs, but Sarah said they were boxers. She had a two-room apartment: she occupied one room and the dogs the other. Around the walls of the dogs' room crates of kibble were stacked to the ceiling. She said the boys devoured it like fiends, and that it took nearly all her salary to support them.

Over drinks, Sarah brought me up to date: when she came to New York, her first job consisted of filing answers from contestants in soap contests—you know, sentences completed in twenty-five words or less. She set up housekeeping with one of her co-workers, who was from Albania originally, and his friends, who were mostly middle Europeans. She did this thinking that was the way most people lived in New York. At least, that's what she told me. She moved when her friend and his companions became involved in a three-day brawl which was finally attended by the police. She was arrested for disorderly conduct and given a suspended sentence. Naturally she lost her job when she did not show up for work or even call in.

Sarah moved into the YWCA until she could find an apartment, but left it and slept in Pennsylvania Station two nights because the YWCA reminded her so much of Mr. and Mrs. Mitchell. She soon found a job as secretary, receptionist, treasurer and librarian for some kind of free-thinkers' organization, and because she could run things the way she wanted with no interference, she was happy with it.

Thus she was when I first met her in New York. I soon renewed contacts with the people ahead of me at the University who had come to New York, and I was admitted to what was known as The Alabama Crowd. I tried to make Sarah go along with me to their parties and gatherings, but she would have none of them. She said those people were a bunch of aging, college-hot snobs and she wouldn't go near them. Finally, I persuaded her to go with me one night, and once there, she had a thoroughly good time, except for one thing: she fell in love again, with a fellow who was the male counterpart of every Beta Nu that ever lived, who gave her a wild spin, and who had not the slightest intention of marrying her. It almost killed her. In fact, she told me she tried sticking her head in the oven, but couldn't keep still because the gas choked her so.

Well, I guess that affair, although brief, was a good thing in a way because it took her mind off those dogs for a while. Now I love dogs and all that, but I don't love boxers in my lap and hugging me around the neck and filling up a tiny apartment. I was not long learning that one unkind word to those beasts meant Sarah in a rage, and *such* rages: I had thought her command of language would recede with time, but I couldn't have been more in error—she had merely expanded her vocabulary to include a choice selection of Yankee indecencies, and you know nothing sounds worse than a New Yorker swearing. She told me her next-door neighbor hated her dogs, and had once threatened to call the police because they were making so much racket. "You can guess what I told *her*," Sarah said.

It did not take me long to discover that Sarah had few, if any, friends. She could be as attractive as the next girl if she wanted to, but let her go out on a date and likely as not she'd gum up the works by getting blind and telling the story of her life before she passed out, thus cancelling anything to her credit. She had no women friends as far as I could tell, and seemed not to want any. For some reason she suffered me, and since I felt sorry for her, I was glad to oblige.

Being Sarah's friend was difficult, however. It meant listening to an endless repetition of her troubles—that is, things that had happened long ago. She had all her misfortunes packaged neatly and the blame affixed, but somehow she could not resist opening them and worrying the contents like her dogs worried their kibble.

She was in the habit of calling me in the middle of the night with Georgine Faircloth's superior connections on her mind, or that time she was jailed overnight in Montgomery because her date ran into another car, or how nasty her father was to her when he paid off her husband. The trouble was, she would keep me up until dawn with some running monologue. When I got tired of it and hung up on her a couple of times she accused me of not giving a damn about what happened to her. I've never seen anybody so obsessed with herself—

Gracious, I've been running on so long about Sarah I almost forgot to tell you what she did. Well, it was one morning a couple of weeks ago. Sarah had a cold and stayed home from the office—at least that's what she said—I think one of those dogs was sick and she was home nursing him. About ten-thirty someone hammered frantically on her door and

Sarah opened it. There was her neighbor, Mrs. Fohlmer, the one Sarah had the run-in with over the dogs, standing in the door. Mrs. Fohlmer had caught herself on fire somehow, probably hot grease, and was in flames, so Sarah shut the door in her face and Mrs. Fohlmer burned to a crisp in the hall.

Now, Sarah keeps calling me up with *that* on her mind. I tell you, it's beginning to get me down.

The VIEWERS *and the* VIEWED

AMONG THE MANY PLEASURES OF living in the Yorkville section of Manhattan is that in the several large motion picture houses interspersed among the sausage establishments, travel agencies, and beer halls of 86th Street, one finds the most subtle and discriminating audiences in the United States.

Bold is the movie company executive who arranges a preview at one of these theatres: before his picture is ten minutes old, there will be no doubt in the executive's mind what the audience thinks of it. Silence is approval; disapproval is expressed by a shower of small unidentifiable objects flung in the direction of the screen, and if one has been foolish enough to sit downstairs one is likely to be inundated by paper bags full of water descending from above. The loges and balconies of these theatres are better organized than any college football cheering section I have ever seen: let one mawkish or fraudulent line, gesture, or sigh be conveyed to the congregations therein, and such unwisdom will be met by several hundred voices replying in even tones, "Aw, come *on*."

I remember one exchange between hero, heroine, and audience that lasted for eleven minutes by my Bulova. For reasons known only to whoever wrote the script, the hero was against sin, drink, the enemy (it was a war picture) and women. If several hundred persons can be said to have groaned in astonishment at such information, let it here be said. Holding these hard views, naturally the hero was confronted with huge doses of everything he was against, and naturally there ensued a scene in which the hero worked himself up to the brink of kissing a young lady of debatable character on the forehead, of all places, and funking it at the last moment. True to the established doctrine of putting a major point across to the masses, the scriptwriter suffered the actors to repeat the business three times. This was a mistake. The first goof met with an organized intake of breath, the second with a sound like air escaping from a tire of International Harvester's biggest tractor, the third with a great double clap-and-stomp the rhythm of which was indiscernible from a single wing T-formation. When our hero finally accomplished what he had no idea of setting out to do, sustained cheering lasted long into the next scene, which, of course, was a battle scene.

No sooner had the audience settled down, than another crisis arose which demanded its comment. The sub-hero, who was meant to be a coward but who did not fool the audience one minute, was confronted with an enemy tank full of the enemy, and he single-handedly dispatched it and its contents with a sedateness that can only emanate from the West Coast. After having been shot at and missed by cannon ball and machine gun bullets from a range not exceeding 20 yards in the aggregate (he used the Old Indian Trick and the Moving Target idea to elude his tormentors), the sub-hero crept up behind the tank and, if anyone will believe me, placed a huge rock in its wheel and rendered it motionless. Then, with cold-bloodedness unequaled since Sherman's march to the sea, this coward opened the hatch of the tank, dropped a live grenade into it, and held it down.

Unscathed by the explosion, the sub-hero strolled casually across a mined area and hoisted his unfortunate brother, the hero, onto his shoulders. The hero had been lying on the ground for some time regretting that he had ever been against sin, drink, the enemy, and women. I think this is correct, because his subsequent gestures seemed to convey that impression. The gestures of the audience were by no means ambiguous: it took the combined authority of the management and two representatives of the police department to restore order.

In the past several months, however, a new game has sprung up in 86th Street which keeps its audiences reasonably attentive to the efforts of the scriptwriters. I'm not sure

I approve of it: it tends to lessen the general fun because the audiences are so busy listening they sometimes forget to watch, but in spite of my efforts to go in the opposite direction, I find myself reluctantly swimming with the tide. I refer to the sport of trying to reconcile the titles of a rash of movies with their subject matter, titles that give one the impression of their having been plucked at random from the Pentateuch by an executive vice-president. Although curious titles have been common attention-getters for centuries, Hollywood cannot fail to accept its share of responsibility in a matter that has gotten out of hand.

The game in 86th Street began with *The High and the Mighty*. It started innocently enough, when several persons including myself overheard this remark in the balcony: "They're all high, but where does the mighty come in?" said a girl to her companion. For the remainder of the picture there was a small island of quiet in the balcony composed of people listening intently to find an answer to her question. We never did.

With each Something and the Something offered on 86th Street, the game gained momentum until now there is absolute unanimity in the higher ranks. We lost the first few matches. Although Hollywood cannot claim credit for it, *The Proud and the Beautiful* eluded everyone, there being nothing in the dialogue, acting, photography, or general tenor of the movie to suggest its title. But Hollywood moved two-up on us with *The Bold and the Brave* and *The Proud and the Profane* and remained so until *The Power and the Prize* came along.

I am happy to say that, according to the rules of the game, *The Power and the Prize* was a success. However, Hollywood tried to swing one across on us by having Mr. Burl Ives remark early in the first quarter, "That's the prize you're going after, son," or something close to it. A large, "*Oh* no," went up from loges and balcony followed by individual comments ranging from, "Interpolation, that's what it is," to, "You got it backwards, Big Daddy."

Complete reconciliation of the picture with its title was a long time coming: quietly and hopefully the audience (the humblest of which takes Haydn and Schumann with his beer) watched a vile-tempered young woman play something terribly classical terribly on the piano, it assimilated unprotestingly a bizarre proposition that the British love pride more than they love money, it was assured that Presbyterians no longer burn people at the stake, and it sat unmoved through some distressing hints that the heroine was a prostitute *and* a communist, until Big Daddy wrapped things up by saying he was a creature of Power.

When this was revealed, jubilation knew no bounds in the balcony. We had won.

But I am afraid that 86th Street audiences are doomed to eventual disappointment. Fewer pictures are coming out with thought-provoking titles: the trend nowadays is to make everything abundantly clear to prospective customers, like *The Ten Commandments*, *Attack*, *The Opposite Sex*. Such titles, I believe, are the result of Hollywood's recurrent cycle of fear that if anything is left to its imagination, the public is somehow less entertained. I trust I have made sufficiently clear the fact that there are more ways of entertaining audiences than are dreamt of in this philosophy.

I notice from *Variety* that there is only one picture in production whose title remains unguessed at. It is called *The Cunning and the Haunted*, and if this title is meant to be the last of its kind, let me prime the pump by respectfully submitting some titles of my own invention with appropriate story-lines. They might keep the game alive and give added enjoyment to the multitudes, who, as we all know, have an average intelligence of twelve-year-old children. I have not registered these titles with any organization, so they are free to anyone who cares to use them:

The Quick and the Dead, a Western

The Knock and the Need, exposé of charity rackets

The Dope and the Fiend, hospital drama

The Block and the Tackle, football story

The Venetian and the Blind, 15th-century costume drama

The Web and the Footed, nature film or title change for *The Thos. Wolfe Story*

The Base and the Vile, murder at the Philharmonic

The Clawed and the Rains, jungle feature

The Good and the Ready, small-town documentary

The Beyond and the Pale, Air Force story

The Pigeon and the Toad, a fable

The Water and the Closet, story-line optional

These suggestions should be enough for Hollywood to mull over for a while, but if they are insufficient, I recommend that the proper motion picture authorities conduct a survey of any 86th Street audience for additional ideas. Their efforts will not go unrewarded.

THIS IS SHOW BUSINESS?

THE ONLY REASON I DID it is because Gerald Gray and his wife are my best friends and I told him I would do it, but I shall never do it again. Become involved with a fashion show, that is. Gerald is vaguely in show business—no, no, no, Gerald *is* in show business; it is I who am vague about what he does: all I know is that he writes and produces fashion shows and he makes a lot of money at it. We never discuss his work, so I had not the faintest idea of what constituted a fashion show until he called me one day and asked if I would help out the girl who does his lighting for him. I was glad to.

By arrangement, I met Clare Waters, the lighting girl, on 9th Avenue in the mid-forties at a curious shop by a police station. Gerald told me that Clare would tell me what to do. I liked her immediately: she was a plump, jolly-looking girl, and she was dressed in charcoal flannel slacks and a green plaid shirt.

"I'm so glad you've come," she said. "I'm afraid you'll be bored stiff with all this, but you'll help a lot if you just wait in the car for me while I do all the errands. You *can* drive, can't you?"

"Yes," I said, "but I've never driven in New York. In fact, I haven't driven a car in several years."

"Oh, I don't think you'll really have to drive at all. I just want somebody to sit in the car in case it has to be moved or I have to leave the engine running. Don't worry about it. Where *is* that truck?"

"What truck?" I asked.

"The truck that's going to take all this." She pointed at a collection of black, box-like instruments that looked like railroad signals. "You see," she said in a low voice, "I'm pulling a fast one."

"Oh," I nodded wisely.

"I've got to get all this into the ballroom without anybody seeing me." She frowned and rubbed her nose.

"Are you stealing it?" I asked.

She shook her head. "It's the union," she said.

Clare walked out of the little shop onto the sidewalk and looked east. She also looked west. I joined her, but I looked at the police station next door.

Several old men loitered with raffish arrogance in front of the station. They are just like the ones at the courthouse in Montgomery, I thought: they managed to convey the impression that although retired, they were still men of affairs. When talking to one another, they cocked their heads importantly to one side; one of them caught sight of Clare and me and said something to his companions, and his companions turned and looked at us. Presently two policemen walked up with two bare-headed men dressed in light suits with heavily padded shoulders.

"They're bringing in people on that acid-throwing case," said Clare. "Let's go back inside."

"I'll watch for the truck," I said.

The old men drew together in a huddle, but dispersed when a patrol car stopped in front of the station and released three more men with heavily padded shoulders. The old men watched them enter the station.

I solved the case: there had not been an acid-throwing in many years, I reasoned. *The Phantom of the Opera* was an acid-throwing case. It was now playing on 86th Street. Therefore, if the police were wise they would do well to comb Yorkville for the culprit, whose inspiration was no doubt drawn from the film. A perfect syllogism.

I was wondering if I should advise the police of this when Clare appeared. "It's three-thirty," she said. "Damn it, I was up until three-thirty this morning."

"Do you have to work like that all the time?" I asked.

"Yes. I spend all day long doing this sort of thing. Waiting for trucks. Then I have to work all night on what I've been waiting all day for."

"Do you suppose I could get back to my apartment by five? I've got to dress and go out for dinner."

"Oh yes. I'll get you back by five. Don't you worry. Why don't you go around the corner and get us some coffee? And bring me a sandwich, will you? I haven't eaten since yesterday."

I walked two blocks before I found a luncheonette. I guessed that she liked ham and her coffee black. This was incorrect, but the man at the lighting shop had some canned milk and a square of sugar which he gave to Clare. She said she didn't mind about the ham, she was so hungry she would eat shoe leather.

When the truck came Clare said, "Now be careful," to the loaders and, "Come on," to me. Clare succeeded in getting the lighting equipment into the ballroom without anyone seeing her, because she did not go near it. We went to a parking lot on 46th Street. She drove her car through the West Side traffic in such a frivolous manner that I kept my eyes shut until we reached 23rd Street and 6th Avenue. She drew up on 23rd Street and stopped the car in front of a sign that indicated we were not to park there after four P.M.

I glanced at my watch. It said five after four, but it always ran fast.

"I won't be gone more than ten minutes," she said. "You'd better sit behind the wheel."

"But the sign—" I said, in some alarm.

"Oh there never are any policemen down here," she said. "If one comes along, just tell him I'll be out in a minute. You know what to do."

"But—"

She was out of the car and on the sidewalk. I watched her disappear inside a doorway. She emerged for a moment and shouted something at me I could not hear, then vanished.

I sat and waited. I watched other cars drive away from the curb until that side of 23rd Street was deserted as far into the distance as I could see.

Naturally, a policeman appeared on a motorcycle. He was clad in a black leather jacket and a squashed-down cap and jodhpurs and puttees. I think he did what is called in show business a double-take, because he rode past Clare's car to the end of the block, stopped abruptly, turned his motorcycle around and headed straight at me.

He came up to the car, touched his cap, and said, "Do you see that sign, Miss?"

Since it was no more than three feet away from me, I said

yes, but I was waiting for a lady who was inside that building. "Is something distressing you?" I asked.

"Can you drive?"

"Yes," I said, "but I have an Alabama license."

The patrolman assumed that anybody who could drive in Alabama could drive in New York: a faulty assumption, I tried to make clear to him, but without success.

"Tell you what you do, lady," he said. "You just circle around the block until she comes out." He kicked at something violently, and his motorcycle sputtered.

He drove away slowly, and in the rear-view mirror I saw him hovering behind the car. Apparently he meant what he said.

When I reached for the gear-shift and trod on the clutch, my right hand closed around nothing and my left foot almost went through the floorboard. The car was one of those push-button affairs where if you know what to do, everything is done for you. I searched the instrument panel hurriedly and found a little rectangle enclosing several knobs over which were engraved N, Dr, R, among other things. I have always been good in an emergency, and I immediately saw that these were the key positions for the gear if there was a gear and that something inside the hood shifted it automatically. I turned on the switch, pressed N, and jammed my foot on the accelerator. The car started and I accelerated briskly. The motor harrumphed in a resentful manner and the car went nowhere.

N for Neutral, I reasoned: R for Ride.

I am sorry to say that R was for Reverse, but I am glad to say that the policeman was no longer behind me. I suppose he was off rounding up other malefactors. Finally, after making a mental note to write to the Chrysler Corporation and gently upbraid them for engineerial ambiguity, I pressed a button which proved to be the correct one and went forward. I drove to the corner of 7th Avenue and 23rd Street, where another policeman told me I could not make a right turn, so I proceeded to where there was no policeman and turned right, then came to the first street on which I could drive east. It was dreadfully narrow.

Now I can drive a car through a sand bed without getting stuck, I can navigate a stumpy pasture without puncturing the gas tank, or I can go like a streak down an open highway, but I cannot drive across a high bridge or down a narrow street without breaking into a sweat and trembling all over.

My hands and forehead were dripping when I returned to where Clare had parked. She was not present. I repeated the circuit, and when I returned the second time I determined, Clare or no Clare, to stop still.

This I did, but I had not been parked five minutes before my friend of the motorcycle was with me again.

He looked sharply at me. "Didn't I tell you to move once?" he inquired.

"You did," I said. "I moved, and now I'm back."

"Lady," he said, "do you want one of these?" He flashed a pad of paper at me.

Suddenly a line from a Victorian school novel occurred to me. It had been rendered with such success that it changed the life of its recipient, so I lowered my eyelids and looked at the steering wheel. "Why do you speak so sharply, sir," I said softly, "when I am doing the best I can?"

This appeal to his better feelings had no effect whatsoever, because he reached in the breast pocket of his leather jacket, drew out a ball-point pen, and began writing on the pad he had waved at me. He was still writing when Clare appeared.

She was carrying a hobo sandwich, half eaten. "Where have you been?" she asked. "What's he doing?"

"Guess," I said.

She took a bite out of the sandwich and went around the car to the policeman. The policeman looked at Clare's jolly face and said, "I don't want to give you a ticket, lady. Will you just get in this car and go. Just go?"

"Sure," she said, and grinned at him. "Thanks, officer!"

"Where *were* you?" I asked, as Clare started the car. "I drove around Manhattan two times waiting for you."

"I didn't see you when I got through, so I just went into that luncheonette—"

We drove by it. The luncheonette was four doors down from the building where Clare had conducted her business.

"—I went in there and got a sandwich," she said. "I'm so upset, and when I'm upset I eat," she added. "I'm a compulsive eater, you know."

"What are you upset about?"

She told me. Costumes.

"I thought you were the lighter," I said.

"Oh yes, but I had to see about this, too. We've got to pick up some scenery right here." She parked the car. We were still on 23rd Street. "It's all these details," she said.

"Clare," I said. "I will not go through this again. You cannot park here."

"It'll just be for a minute. They're on the ground floor."

We were saved by a blond young man who came out of the building and waved us away. "They'll give you a ticket like a shot," he said. "Go down to the corner, turn right, and idle your motor. They'll let you stand."

A Negro man and the blond young man carried some

long, thin pieces of scenery and tied them to the top of the car with light rope. "That'll hold," said the Negro man. "If it doesn't, you'll find out."

"Thanks, Boyd," said Clare. "What time is it?"

My watch said four-fifty.

"Don't worry," she said. "I'll get you back by five."

I don't know why she did it, but Clare headed east at her first opportunity, came to 3rd Avenue and drove up it until she reached 42nd Street; then she turned west on 42nd Street until she came to Broadway, where she turned north.

"There's a little place over here that makes the best egg-and-tomato sandwiches in New York," she said, "if I can find it. I've got to make a phone call to tell those people to stay open until I get there. I think they stay open until five-thirty but I'm not sure."

"Where are they?" I asked.

"Ninety-First and First," she said. "Here's the place."

She parked at a bus stop.

"Clare—"

"Oh don't be so jumpy," she said.

When I am upset I do not eat, I cross my arms and clutch them to me. When I thought I would do this I discovered that my arms were already crossed and I was clutching.

The traffic was appalling. A bus rolled up and swerved to keep from hitting the car, and I did not look at the driver or his passenger.

When Clare returned she was bearing an egg sandwich and good news. "They'll stay open," she said.

Somehow we got to Central Park, but not before Clare nearly hit a man with a horse and a hansom cab who shouted, "Damnation!" at her. She was having trouble driving and keeping the egg in her sandwich.

"Is it this sort of thing that upsets you?" I asked.

"Driving? Oh no, it's this job. I don't know why I got into it. So many little details. I'll be up all night again tonight. Do you have any nephews?"

"Three," I said.

"Well I've got a new one. He's two weeks old and I haven't seen him yet. My brother lives just eight blocks away from me."

We came to a confusing place in the park where several roads meet. Clare shut her eyes and drove forward. Safely across, she opened them again and said, "I always do that. Never fails. No, it's all these little things. Lord, I'm still hungry."

"Do you smoke?" I asked. "That might—"

“Oh no. Filthy habit,” she said. “I’m sorry—”

I was lighting a fresh cigarette from the stump of my old one. “That’s all right,” I said.

“Where do you live?”

“Eighty-First and York.”

“Good,” she said. “I can let you off at Eighty-Sixth and Third and then shoot on up to Ninety-First.”

“Excellent,” I said.

When she pulled up to the corner of 86th and Lexington, she said, “Thanks so much for helping me out. You don’t know what a help you’ve been. Can I call on you again?”

“Any time,” I said.

“What time is it?” she asked.

“Five-twenty,” I said.

“Good! They’ll still be there. See you!” She waved and was gone.

The walk did me no good. When I got to my flat I went to the bathroom, put the stopper in the tub, and turned on the hot water tap. I went to the kitchen cabinet and took out a bottle of bourbon and a glass. I filled the glass half full of whiskey, returned to the bathroom, and set it on the edge of the tub. I went to the livingroom and pulled a book from the shelves: *A Forty Years’ Friendship: Letters from the Late Henry Scott Holland to Mrs. Drew*. I carried it to the bathroom, put it beside the glass of whiskey, and took off my clothes. I cut the boiling water with cold until it was bearable, got in the tub and drank my whiskey and read my book:

> I am overwhelmed with horror. A rumour came through the Clives, I think, that Mrs. Gladstone said that Mr. Gladstone wanted to see a sermon of mine—and, actually, my credulous family believed this, and my sister has written the thing out and actually sent it to Hawarden. . . . The very picture of this presumption fills me with alarm and indignation.
>
> I can only appeal to you. Could you secrete and remove it?

No, never again. Not even for Gerald Gray.

The

CAT'S MEOW

WHEN OUR PARENTS DIED MY sister, an old-maid lawyer, sold our house and built another one in a new section of town called by its inhabitants The Ridge. It was just as well, because Doe foresaw difficulty in managing both the old house and her law practice—one would decline, and anyone who knew Doe would have no trouble guessing which. The new house was just like her: there was a reason for each of its peculiarities. It was Georgian in style, but there was a breezeway from garage to kitchen: one drop of rain and Doe caught cold. There were Dutch doors in front, rear, and on the side screen porch: if Doe wished to wander on hot Sunday afternoons in her pajama tops she was assured of God's fresh air and her privacy. The kitchen was enormous, old-fashioned (she wouldn't have an electric stove in the house) but as well organized as one of her Supreme Court briefs. Although sudden draughts brought on the arthritis in her shoulder (her doctor said they didn't; Doe said her doctor didn't have arthritis) there was a big attic fan in the hallway she turned on for guests. Whenever Doe sat down her feet automatically sought a resting place several inches above the floor, so there were ottomans in front of every chair in the livingroom.

Doe did not love her new house. She loved only three things in this world: the study and practice of law, camellias, and the Methodist Church. She was an authority on each. Time spent on pursuits other than these was time wasted, which was why I always felt the fifteen years' difference in our ages when she was obliged to rise at two-thirty in the morning and meet me in Mobile when I made my yearly journey home. When I walked down the ramp at the airport, I always felt vaguely apprehensive lest I encounter her furious eyes and stern mouth as I used to when I was a child and she would drag me out of the picture show at an ungodly hour. Of course I never did. She was always delighted to see me, and this made me glad because I loved her dearly.

In the two hours it takes to drive from Mobile to Maycomb, Doe would bring me up to date on the whole town, then she would proceed to camellias, the Wesleyan Service Guild, and her current legal problems. Land titles and the laws of taxation have never fascinated me, but such was Doe's gift of narrative that I would always forget she drove too fast, that she was in the habit of peering hard at anything on the roadside which struck her fancy, and that she hugged the right side of the highway with such tenacity should she ever have a wreck, it would be because she obeyed the law with too much firmness.

When I last rode to Maycomb with her Doe stayed on camellias all the way. No, it is better to say that camellias this time involved Arthur, her new yard man, who pleased her, which was a revelation. She had lived on The Ridge less than a year, had gone through four yard men, and had reduced them finally to mere lawn-cutters, allowing not one black hand to touch her shrubs.

"I can't wait for you to watch him work," she said. "He's completely different from anybody who ever put a hand on that yard. You don't have to tell him a thing, you don't have to hang over him a minute. First day he came to work he had the whole lawn mowed by noon, and when I got home from the office he was watering my camellias. The hair rose on my head, but when I inspected the damage I found he'd pruned 'em all and didn't scar a *one*. After that—well, I let him run wild. I don't have to tell him to do one thing, whatever needs doing in that yard he just goes about his business and does it. Isn't that the end?"

Doe looked at me so long I said, "Yes," to keep her on the road.

"He's the only Negro I've ever talked to who understands what I'm saying when I say it. Now I want to tell you something, Baby," she said. "Arthur takes considerable getting used to."

"Getting used to?"

"Yes," said Doe. "He's a Yankee."

"A what?" I said.

"A Yankee. A Yankee Negro."

"In Maycomb? At home?"

"Yes." Doe nodded complacently. She always liked to try to shock me, and this time she did. "He has as much education as you have."

"Hoo," was all I could say. Perhaps he was a deaf-mute. Or maybe he was an NAACP organizer: if he was, what a good one on Doe, I thought.

"He came from somewhere in Pennsylvania originally," Doe said. "Joe and Alice Lindley found him down around Abbott County and offered him a job on their place. He lives in a little room Joe built onto their garage and works four days a week for them. I have him over one day a week and the Cleburnes one."

She gave me a full minute to think this over.

"Now, Baby," she said, "he's going to take a bit of getting used to. You have to put him in his place occasionally, but do it nicely, now. Don't let him make you mad. He's not like any Negro you ever knew before."

I refrained from reminding Doe that for the past seven years I had lived in New York City, where among other things more than eight million people enjoy the benefits of democracy.

But I'll be damned if he didn't. Not make me mad, but I was downright uncomfortable around him. If we were only in New York and not in Maycomb, Alabama, I wouldn't have batted an eye at him.

He was an oddity. His bearing was not that of studied, deliberate humility like the graduates' of Tuskegee Institute, but if he had been in the least bit arrogant, if he had worn his education like his Sunday suit—if, like the rest of them these days, he had been careful to look me squarely and self-consciously in the eye when he addressed me, I would not have felt a twinge.

Instead, Arthur stayed well within all Southern boundaries; he conformed to the spirit as well as the letter of them not, it seemed, because they were Southern but because they were determined by the simple courtesy one being shows another, and were in no way connected with anybody's interpretation of the Constitution.

Arthur loved Doe's yard. He kept the grass cut with a Navy trim; he had on his own initiative made a zinnia bed in a far corner of the back lot; he and Doe started a complicated grafting job from which Arthur emerged with the upper hand. The days he worked for the Lindleys, even, no sun set that did not find him watering Doe's camellias. He liked Doe; he liked to work for her, and Doe was good to him. Every Wednesday he borrowed a dollar from her on his Friday's pay to go to the picture show; occasionally he popped through the hedge dividing Doe's and the Lindleys' yards to ask Doe if he could cut some gladioli for his evening's date. Doe said he courted the colored teachers and enjoyed social superiority among the Maycomb Negroes. "It's because he's half white," she said.

Indeed he was: he was light brown, with a straight nose, a thin mouth and jug ears. He was slightly bandy-legged and his hair was going gray. I guessed he was in his early fifties.

One evening he appeared at the kitchen door and asked if Doe was there. I called her, and he said, "Miss Doe, I want to show you some pictures of my family."

Doe spent ten minutes admiring his relatives. One went to Cornell or somewhere, another was in the Air Force, I think. They were small-boned, intelligent-looking people.

Doe was right: Arthur took considerable getting used to. Doe said it was because I couldn't adjust myself to an emancipated Negro at such close quarters and that it proved no matter how long I lived away from home I would always be from Maycomb, Alabama, to which I preserved an uncharacteristic silence, for Doe was a deep-water segregationist, I was not, and the last thing I wanted was a row which would separate me from the only family I had left. I suppose a lot of people like me have mastered the first lesson of living at home these days: if you don't agree with what you hear, place your tongue between your teeth and bite hard.

Arthur made me nervous because he left so much to be said. Aside from scaring the life out of me by sometimes appearing unexpectedly, silently, at the back door, he seemed to have the best intentions in the world. I tried to explain my feeling to Doe one night. "It's because he's *here*," I said. "Why did he choose to come here? It's like you decided to start throwing ashes on yourself, or to try picking up a load that's too heavy for you. Why did he come down here when he knows what it's like?"

"Maybe he's one of those rare souls who knows what's good for him," she said. "Maybe he likes this kind of living better than dog-eat-dog. We don't hate colored people down here, you know."

"You mean he prefers benevolent despotism? I doubt that."

"I'd rather live here in peace than in the race-riot country," said Doe.

I warded off a lecture on the evils of Detroit by asking, "What do you really know about him?"

"No more than what I've already told you, and what he's said about his home. He's been here six months without a moment's trouble. If Joe Lindley says he's all right, that's enough for me. What does anybody ever know about Negroes?"

My mouth was open to reply but I shut it and went to bed.

When I had been home nearly two weeks, Doe had some title work in Mobile which would keep her there several days, and I accompanied her with the intention of sunning myself on the beach at Dauphin Island. We stayed in Mobile from Monday to Saturday: it rained on us every day, I didn't go near the beach, Doe was fractious because she did not finish her abstract, and to crown it all the weeds were a foot high in the front yard when we got home.

The Lindleys were not even speaking to Arthur: he had gone to Selma for a five-day weekend without saying one word to anybody. Alice Lindley was so angry she shook when she told Doe and me about it, but Joe said, "They all have to break loose once in a while."

Arthur was sheepish, Doe was amused by his escapade, and I was puzzled. Because the Lindleys preserved a staunch silence for several days, Arthur sought out Doe for some form of human contact. He would never come to me. I saw them several times standing in the yard together, and once when I asked Doe what they were talking about, Doe said she had told Arthur she wanted to start a narcissus bed next spring, and Arthur had said, "Narcissus. That's the boy who looked at himself in the pool." Doe said she intended to cling to him with hoops of steel, that she had never seen one like him and never would again.

"What if he ups and leaves?" I asked. "He could be making four times as much money as he does around here."

"I doubt about him leaving," said Doe.

But he did.

It was a week later on Sunday afternoon that Joe Lindley came over and asked to speak to Doe. Joe was a shy sort of fellow, so I asked him if he wished to see her privately.

"No, you might be interested in this. Doe," he said, when she appeared, "I want to talk some with you about Arthur. He's gone."

Doe sat down on the sofa. "Sit down, Joe," she said.

Joe wrapped his legs around an ottoman, rubbed the back of his head and said, "I don't know exactly how to start."

"Begin when you found him," said Doe.

"Well first of all, Doe, I gave Arthur my word I wouldn't tell anyone about this, but after what he did I think I certainly owe you an explanation, and everyone he's worked for. I've been in a right peculiar position about him. I've wanted to tell you but I gave him my word I wouldn't, so there it is."

"Of course, Joe. I understand," said Doe.

"Yes. Well," Joe said, and stopped. He began again: "You see, he's been out of the penitentiary on parole to me for the past six months."

Doe grinned. "I thought it was something like that," she said. "He had all the earmarks."

"You don't miss a trick, do you?"

"It's my business not to," she said. "Go on."

"He was visiting some relatives down here and they all got high one night and tried to break into a store. Their old car died on 'em before they went two feet and they were picked up. Arthur got the book. He was from the north and he didn't know how to behave in front of a judge. That was twenty years ago."

"He was in prison for twenty years?" The faint twin lines between Doe's eyebrows sprang taut.

"Twenty years."

"That seems hard for a routine breaking-and-entering. Are you telling me all the facts?" The lawyer in Doe was rising.

"Yes. He came up for parole in February. Jemson, he's the camp warden, said Arthur was the smartest colored man he'd ever seen. I was off hunting with Jemson one weekend, that's how I found him. Our place was getting too much for Alice to cope with by herself, and Jemson was interested in starting Arthur off on the right foot when he came up for parole. Jemson said Arthur was the cat's meow, said the Yankees educated him and the guards taught him his place."

"Yes," said Doe flatly.

"Now I made it clear to him in the beginning that I was going to some expense to take him on, what with building that room for him. I told him I wasn't having any congregating in the back, and no drinking, and he could come on those terms or stay in the pen. He'd be my responsibility and I wasn't about to have him disrupting the neighborhood."

Joe stirred and rearranged himself on the ottoman. "You know as well as I do he had the most perfect setup anybody in his fix ever had. Alice even taught him how to make beds."

Joe kicked the ottoman out from under him and stood up. "I should have seen it coming. It was when I bought that old huntin' car. First time he saw it he asked me if I'd sell it to him. Always after me about it, always wanted me to take it out of his pay every week and you know, he couldn't even drive."

"What did he intend to do with it?" asked Doe.

"His friends would drive him."

Doe sighed.

"The thing that galls me, though," said Joe, "is I told him if he stayed here two years and kept his record clean, all of us would try to get him a pardon."

"I'd have done it for him," said Doe. "But what made him up and leave?"

"It was when he went AWOL that week. Too much for him. He said, 'Mr. Lindley, I rode all the way to Selma in a Buick.'"

We were all silent. Joe chewed on his upper lip with his bottom teeth. Finally he said, "Lord knows, Doe, I told him. I told him if he left this neighborhood all he needed was one false move and he'd be back in the pen for the rest of his life. He needs just one wreck, just one carload of Negroes, and it's goodbye Arthur. They'd kill him. He's got some wild idea of working in a restaurant in Selma."

"Have you talked to the parole officer?"

"I've told the parole officer until I'm blue in the face it's the worst thing on earth that could happen to him. You know what he did?"

"Who? The parole officer?"

"No. Arthur. Made up some tale about how I was fixing to get rid of him anyway and told the parole officer so he'd have to find another place. Right behind my back!"

"That's typical," said Doe. "They'll do anything to get what they want."

"A pardon, so he could go anywhere in the world, a job and a good home for the rest of his life. What else could anybody want?"

"His own kind," said Doe. "He was rather isolated here. It never comes out of 'em."

Joe moved toward the door. "Well, that's that. I've got to go tell the rest of The Ridge about him. They'll fling a fit." He nodded goodbye to me.

"Couldn't you make him stay?" asked Doe.

"Not a chance," he said. "He's got nothing but car on his mind."

"Like children," said Doe.

"You know what he said to me before he left? He said, 'I'm sorry, Mr. Lindley, I got to have some fun before I get too old to enjoy it.' He said, 'In five years I'll be sixty, and that's too old to enjoy anything.'"

Doe shook her head. "No thought for the future," she said. "No plan for living at all." She sighed again. "I'd hoped he was really different. He can't help it, Joe. Don't blame Arthur. He's just a Negro, that's all, and he can't help being one."

It was beginning to rain, and she shut the front door behind Joe. She returned to the livingroom, raised her eyebrows at me, and grimaced. She picked up the *Montgomery Advertiser*, sat down, and began reading it from back to front, as was her custom.

"Doe?" I said presently.

"What?" she said. She looked around the corner of the paper at me. I suddenly felt ten years old again.

"Nothing," I said.

She resumed reading.

The

LAND *of*

SWEET FOREVER

IT IS A TRUTH GENERALLY acknowledged by the citizens of Maycomb, Alabama, that a single woman in possession of little else but a good knowledge of English social history must be in want of someone to talk to. This became evident to Maycomb after she had been home less than a week; it was evident to her after two days that she could not with any success sustain fifteen minutes' pleasantry with people she had merely known all her life without drying up stone dead. This defect, she thought, stemmed mainly from her inability to produce a suitable reply to the question, "Well, how's New York?", a question which inevitably and immediately followed a report on the condition of whomever she happened to be talking to, and which was thrust at her with the suddenness of a lateral pass.

The summer would have been bearable had her family chosen to communicate with her, but her father and sister were up to their ears in a timberland transaction, and they afforded her preoccupied, good-natured sniffs in answer to anything she said, which melded into outright irritation if she persisted in any conversational gambit that might demand two minutes' consecutive thought. The persons to whom, in childhood's secret society, she had pledged undying loyalty had long since married and were rearing children, an undertaking which seemed to sap all their energy and imagination. The generation ahead of her, with children beyond whipping age, devoted its time to the acquisition of electrical appliances. There was no pleasure, even, in looking at the town itself: the Maycomb of her childhood was one thing; Maycomb today is dotted with neon vulgarity and hundreds of small new houses a baby tornado with one breath could reduce to swirls of trash. So she devoted the summer to the only institutions she found more or less unchanged: Maycomb's golf course, which she cultivated silently for three months, and its Methodist Church, where she went every Sunday and sang hymns at the top of her voice.

There is nothing like a blood-curdling hymn to make one feel at home. All sense of isolation withers and dies in the presence of some two hundred sinners earnestly requesting to be plunged beneath a red, redeeming flood. While offering to the Lord the results of Mr. Cowper's hallucination, or declaring it was Love that lifted her, Jean Louise shared the warmness that prevails among diverse individuals who climb into the same boat for one hour each week.

She was totally unprepared for what happened immediately after collection on the Sunday before the Friday she was due to return to New York. Maycomb Methodists sing what they call The Doxology in lieu of the minister praying over the collection plate to spare him the rigors involved in inventing yet another prayer, since by that time he has uttered three healthy invocations. From the time of her earliest ecclesiastical recollection, Maycomb Methodists had sung The Doxology in one way and in one way only:

Praise—God—from—whom—all—blessings—flow, a rendition as much a part of Southern Methodist ritual as the Burial Service. That Sunday, the congregation were innocently clearing their throats to drag it accordingly when out of a cloudless sky Mrs. Clyde Haskew crashed down on the organ

> PraiseGodfromwhomall Bles—sings Flo—w
> PraiseHimallcreatures He-re Bee—low
> PraiseHimaboveye Heavn—ly Ho—sts
> PraiseFatherSonand Ho—ly Gho—st!

In the confusion that followed, if the Archbishop of Canterbury had materialized in full regalia she would not have been in the least surprised. The congregation had failed to notice any change in Mrs. Haskew's lifelong interpretation, and they intoned The Doxology to its bitter end as they had been reared to do, while Mrs. Haskew romped madly ahead like something out of Salisbury Cathedral.

Her first thought was that Henry Hackett had lost his mind. Henry Hackett had been music director of the Maycomb Methodist Church for as long as she could remember. He was a big, good man with a gentle baritone, who ruled a choir of repressed soloists with easy tact, and who had an iron-clad memory for the favorite hymns of District Superintendents. In the sundry church wars that seem to be a living part of Methodist faith, Henry could be counted on as the one person to keep his head, giving advice when asked for it, and reconciling the more primitive elements of the congregation with the Young Turk faction. He had devoted thirty years' spare time to his church, and his church had recently rewarded him with a trip to a Methodist music camp in South Carolina.

Her second impulse was to blame it on the minister. He had long been suspected of liberal tendencies; he was too friendly, some thought, with his Yankee brethren; he had recently emerged somewhat damaged from a controversy over the Apostles' Creed; and worst of all, he was thought to be ambitious. She was building up an airtight case against him which was promptly canceled when she remembered he was tone-deaf. So she returned to Henry and stared straight at him for the remainder of the service. She decided he was not sick, just tired, but in spite of her efforts to quell it she felt amusement turning to indignant displeasure. How dare he change it? Was he trying to lead them back to the Mother Church? Just precisely what did he think he was doing? Had she allowed reason to rule, she would have realized that Henry Hackett, who runs a cotton warehouse six days a week with great exactitude, had little taste or talent for ritualistic niceties. Whatever his motive, it was pure. But however pure, she thought him on dangerous ground indeed, if on any ground at all, for Methodism is notoriously short on theology and long on good works.

The minister pronounced the benediction and was on his way to the door when she apprehended Henry, who had remained behind to shut the windows. She noticed that she was not the first: he was already in conversation with a tall young man whose face belonged to the Wade family, but whose body showed extensive Talbert influence. He was Talbert Wade, of course. She had not seen him since he was a child.

". . . shouldn't do it like that, Mr. Hackett," he was saying. "We are Methodists."

She listened to young Talbert's reasons why Mr. Hackett shouldn't do it like that. They were sound. Henry interrupted Talbert and introduced them.

"Young man," she said, "you have either been to church in England or you watched the Coronation on television with considerable acuteness. Which is it?"

"Both," he said, and grinned delightedly.

"Henry?" she said.

Henry threw up his hands as if to ward off whatever was coming.

"Don't look at me," he said. "It's the way they told us to sing it at Camp Charles Wesley."

"You aren't going to take something like that lying down, are you?" she said. "*Who* told you to do that?"

"The music instructor. He was from New Jersey. He taught a class in what was wrong with Southern church music."

"He did, did he?"

"Yes."

"What did he say was wrong with it?"

"He said we might as well be singing, 'Stick your snout under the spout where the Gospel comes out,' as most of the things we sing. Said they ought to ban Fanny Crosby by church law and that 'Rock of Ages' was an abomination unto the Lord."

"Oh?"

"He said we ought to pep up The Doxology."

"Pep it up? How?"

"Like we sang it today."

She sat down in the front pew. Apparently, she thought, our brethren in the northland are not content merely with the Supreme Court's activities: they are now trying to change our hymns on us.

Henry said, "He told us we ought to get rid of the Southern hymns and learn some other ones. I don't like it—ones he suggested don't even have tunes."

"Southern hymns?" she said. "Now, Henry, let's analyze this. Let's see now, he wants us to sing The Doxology down the line with nothing less than the Church of England, but then he turns square around and wants to throw out—'Abide with Me'?"

"Right."

"Lyte. What about 'When I Survey the Wondrous Cross'?"

"That's another one," said Henry. "He gave us a list, and I think that's on it."

"Gave you a list, did he? I suppose 'Onward, Christian Soldiers' is included?"

"At the top," said Henry.

"H.F. Lyte, Isaac Watts, Sabine Baring-Gould." She permitted herself the luxury of rolling out the last name in

Maycomb County accents: long a's, i's, and a pause between syllables. It felt wonderful. "Every one an Englishman, Henry, good and true. Wants to throw them out but sing The Doxology like we were all in Westminster Abbey, does he? Well let me tell you something—"

She looked up at Henry, who was nodding agreement, and at Talbert Wade, who had stood so silently all the while she had forgotten he was there.

"Your man's a snob, Henry, and that's a fact."

"He was sort of a sissy," said Henry.

"I'll bet he was. Are you going along with all this nonsense?"

"Heavens no," he said. "I thought I'd try it once, just to make sure of what I'd already guessed. Congregation'll never learn it. Besides, I like the old ones."

"So do I, Henry," she said.

She rose to go. "Well, goodbye. I'll see you this time next year. I'm leaving this coming Friday."

They shook hands under cover of his soft farewell phrases. She nodded to Talbert, and was halfway across the churchyard when she turned and discovered Talbert at her heels.

"Can I give you a lift?" she asked.

"No thanks. I have my own car."

As she slid under the steering wheel she noticed he was still hovering. He was a nice-looking child, combining the best elements of the Talberts and the Wades. He was perhaps twenty-one years old.

"Would it be all right if I came to see you this afternoon?" he said.

"Of course," she said, and changed her mind. There would be few golf-playing days left, and she resented giving up her Sunday afternoon routine to entertain the young. She contemplated him somewhat gloomily: he would be full of Europe—he looked suspiciously as if he had returned from a tour and had picked up a Brooks Brothers suit on the way home. He was obviously intelligent, but he would have only just emerged from the comatose cocoon of his teens into that age of fierce brightness where every human emotion is examined and carefully labeled; he would be wise, he would be overwhelmingly definite, he would be appalling, and she would be rude.

He sensed her annoyance. "I wouldn't be breaking up your afternoon, would I?" he said.

"Of course not," she said. "You drink coffee, don't you? Good."

She drove home. Her father and sister were in Mobile that weekend, and she was alone in the house. She ate lunch on the kitchen table, changed into slacks, worked herself into a bad humor, and had just collapsed on the porch lounger when the doorbell rang.

Talbert had wasted no time. He greeted her with a kind of assurance she found odd in a Maycomb boy. His manners were as easy and graceful as his long-legged lope. She began to feel better, then worse: he was probably incurably in love with himself.

"I thought I would die in church this morning," he said, as he sat down.

She thought longingly of the golf course, and of how much pleasure she found in the crisp click of a ball well hit. With what she hoped was invisible effort, she tried to organize her feelings into some semblance of fair-mindedness: give the boy a chance, she thought. Give the child a chance.

"I thought I would curl up and die," Talbert amended, when she did not answer him immediately.

"You seem to have recovered," she said politely. "What are you majoring in?"

"Economics," he said, which was sufficient to make her abandon any generous impulses she may have had about carrying her share of the load.

"Then I'm afraid we are in for a High Evangelical afternoon," she murmured.

"What?" he said.

"I said I'm afraid we are in for a High Evangelical afternoon."

If his hide was pierced he did not show it; thus her own bad behavior came home to roost. She said, "You know how Maycomb is. There's not a thing to do in this town on Sunday but read *Holy Living and Dying.*"

"Yes," he said, grinning at her. "I've been home a week now, and I'm already feeling like Augustus J.C. Hare."

"What?" she said.

"I said I've—"

"I beg your pardon, Talbert, I heard you the first time—"

She looked at him sharply. He had not quite become a man: his face and hands were smooth, as yet unset by the mold of maturity.

"—I was just wondering out of what rarefied firmament you snatched Augustus J.C. Hare?"

"You slay me the way you talk sometimes," said Talbert. "This morning—"

"I shall be more disposed to slay you if you don't tell me what the hell you know about Augustus J.C. Hare," she said grimly.

"Oh *you* know." The boy raised his hands lazily, palms upward, and let them fall in his lap. "He got mixed up with all those Maurices when he was a child and they put him in back braces and clamps and snatched his dinner out from under him in case he developed gluttony and were always sending for Uncle Julius to come over and pull him out from under the bed. Uncle Julius married a Maurice, you know, and she was Augustus's adopted mother's best friend so he was brought up an Evangelical and the poor old soul was thirty-five before—"

For the second time that Sunday she was stunned to silence.

"—before he—ah, you know—and every time it happened he put a big black cross in his journal!"

Somewhat hastily, she told Talbert she would get the coffee. Safely in the kitchen, she doubled over the sink with silent laughter. In some confusion, she attempted to sift Talbert's narrative for his source material: Hare's memoirs, of course, but she had a dim recollection that the last fact was in one of Somerset Maugham's more obscure essays. *Well*, she thought.

But she served Talbert coffee without comment. She was far from trusting him: this was probably Talbert's set piece of entertainment for older women, and she was positive he regarded her as an advanced case of caducity. She had met many of his kind; they could be found in abundance sitting on the edges of sofas in Upper East Side apartments. She decided to tackle him, stomp on him, and get it over with quickly. There would still be time for eighteen holes before sundown.

"You remember when Uncle Julius got engaged?" she asked casually, bringing her heavy artillery to the front.

Talbert looked at a distant light-pole. "'It was the most dismal of betrothals,'" he quoted. "'Esther sobbed and cried, my mother sobbed and cried, Uncle Julius sobbed and cried daily. I used to see them sitting holding each other's hands and crying on the banks of the Rotha.' That's in the first volume."

"You young fiend," she said.

Talbert wallowed like a puppy in the waves of her approval.

"What on earth made you memorize *The Story of My Life*?" she said. "You seem to be athletic enough."

"I loved it when I read it."

"That is no answer. What else have you read? This kind of thing, I mean."

"Don't look at me like that and I'll try to tell you."

She was one of those people who, when registering approbation, look furious, and she was unaware until then that she had pinned Talbert to his chair like a moth. She released him with the most cordial smile she could muster, and he relaxed.

"I'm so sorry," she said. "Do go on."

"Well, you might say that the Victorians are a sort of hobby of mine. I've read everything about them I can get my hands on."

"Oh? And what plunged you into the 19th century?"

"I was homesick."

"*Home*sick?"

"You know, I've been at Northwestern for three years now. It's different up there. You know how it is. Well, Mamma and Daddy said I'd drink up the earth at Alabama so they made me go to Northwestern. At first it was hell but it began to wear off. Well, I had to read Strachey's *Victoria*—isn't that the greatest thing you ever read?"

"No," she said.

"Well, anyway I had to read it for a lit course and it reminded me so much of Maycomb one thing led to another, you know."

"Reminded you so much of Maycomb?"

Talbert nodded. "The families and things. All the yapping that went on—"

"The families and things?"

"Yes. You know, how everybody was or almost was kin to everybody else. It's just like here in Maycomb County."

"Talbert," she said, with formidable patience, "how can someone be almost kin to somebody else?"

"Well, you know. Let's see now. You remember Frank Buckland, don't you?"

In spite of herself, she was being drawn into Talbert Wade's fantastical world: "You mean the naturalist? The one who carried dead fish around in his suitcase and kept a jackal in his rooms?"

"That's the one. You remember Matthew Arnold, don't you?"

She said she did.

"Well, Frank Buckland was Matthew Arnold's father's sister's husband's brother's son, so that made them almost kin. See?"

"Yes, but—"

Talbert squinted at a red geranium in the corner of the porch. "Didn't your brother," he said slowly, "marry his great-uncle's son's wife's second cousin?"

She clapped her hands over her eyes and thought hard. "He did," she finally said. "Talbert, I think you have made a non sequitur but I'm not at all positive."

"Well it's all the same thing, really."

She said anybody who could straighten out the Arnolds

and Bucklands in one breath deserved either some kind of plaque or to be shut up. In an asylum, she added. "Furthermore, Talbert," she said, "I have done a little more than dabble in your subject for over fifteen years, and I have so far failed to see any connection with Maycomb, Alabama."

"That's because you haven't looked," he said.

"Well, I must confess that I did not have Maycomb on my mind when exploring the Oxford Movement."

"You and Mr. Hackett reminded me vividly of it this morning," said Talbert. "I'll betcha it began just like that."

She told Talbert that the starting whistle for the Oxford Movement was blown by the Rev. John Keble on July 14, 1833, in a sermon entitled *National Apostasy*, a copy of which lay somewhere in her apartment in New York; she would be delighted to mail it to him for his inspection, and she challenged him to find anything in it that could possibly remind him of this morning's proceedings. She spoke harshly, because in the deepest recesses of her consciousness she knew she was on losing ground: this boy was somehow outrageously right, insanely correct in his comparisons. She crushed viciously a sudden impulse to regard the Noetic brethren as a sextet of fiddlers with the Provost of Oriel calling the tune.

"—somebody in Maycomb who's really the living counterpart of every Victorian who drew a breath. You remember old Dean Stanley, don't you?"

"I'm sorry, Talbert?"

"You remember old Dean Stanley, don't you?"

"Yes." The absent-minded, fluff-haired little clergyman and his stalwart Lady Augusta drifted gently into her mind, and she braced herself for Talbert's remarks.

"Doesn't he remind you of Mr. Finckney Sewell?"

"Certainly not," she said.

"Oh you know, when Stanley was Dean of Westminster he dug up nearly everybody in the Abbey looking for James the Second, or was it James the First?"

"Oh my God," she said. During the depression, Mr. Fink Sewell, a Maycomb resident long noted for his independence of mind, disentombed his own grandfather and extracted all his gold teeth to pay off a mortgage. When the sheriff apprehended him for grave-robbery and gold-hoarding, Mr. Fink demurred on the theory that if his own granddaddy wasn't his, whose was he? The sheriff said old Mr. M.F. Sewell was in the public domain, but Mr. Fink said huffily he supposed it was his lot, his granddaddy, and his teeth, and declined forthwith to be arrested. The consensus of opinion in Maycomb was that Mr. Fink was an honorable man, he was trying his best to pay his debts, and he remained unmolested by the law.

"Of course, Dean Stanley had the highest historical motives for his excavations," she said, and planted her feet firmly on the floor lest she should rise to the ceiling and fly away.

"Yes," replied Talbert, "but their minds worked exactly alike. You can't deny he invited every heretic he could lay his hands on to preach in the Abbey. You remember how he supported Bishop Colenso."

She remembered. Bishop Colenso, whose views on everything were considered unsound in that day, was the little dean's particular pet, and when the Bishop was in danger of being unfrocked, Stanley made a ringing Convocation speech in his defense, asking that body was it aware that Colenso was the only colonial bishop who had bothered to translate the Bible into Zulu, which was rather more than the rest had done.

"Mr. Fink was just like him," said Talbert. "Mamma says one night in church he testified how liquor had ruined him just to help out the drys, and she says he never touched a drop in his life. She says he subscribed to *The Wall Street Journal* in the middle of the depression and dared anybody to say a word about it. Mr. Jeddo at the post office nearly had a spasm every time he put the mail up."

She stared at Talbert. The Wades had been friends of her

family for generations—almost kin, she reflected wryly. The mind, the heart, the actions of any given Wade were as predictable to her as the days of the week: all Wades followed a tribal trail of integrity, dullness, and cotton-buying. Talbert was some antic mutation.

"—just like him," Talbert was saying. "Or take Harriet Martineau—"

Her mind leapt frantically to the Lake District, hovered a while, and settled with uncertainty upon the works of Mrs. Humphry Ward. "Didn't Mrs. Humphry Ward say she never could remember whether Miss Martineau was a mesmeristic atheist or an atheistic mesmerist?" she asked, trying to get back into the swim of things.

"I don't know, but do you remember Mrs. E.C.B. Franklin?"

She did, and groped through the years for a comparison. History is comparatively silent on Miss Martineau's accoutrements, but Mrs. E.C.B.'s were easy to remember: crocheted tam, crocheted dress through which peeped pink crocheted drawers, and crocheted stockings. Every Saturday Mrs. E.C.B. walked three miles to town from her farm, which was called Cape Jessamine Copse. Mrs. E.C.B. wrote poetry; so did Harriet Martineau.

Talbert said, "Remember the minor women poets?"

"Yes," she said.

"Mrs. E.C.B. was all of 'em rolled into one."

"Yes, Talbert."

When she was a child she devilled for a while at the *Maycomb County Tribune* office and witnessed several altercations, including the last, between Mrs. E.C.B. and Mr. Underwood. Mr. Underwood was an old-time printer and stood for no nonsense. He worked all day at a vast black linotype, refreshing himself at intervals from a gallon jug containing harmless cherry wine. One Saturday Mrs. E.C.B. stalked into the office with an effusion Mr. Underwood said he refused to disgrace the *Tribune* with: it was a cow obituary in verse, beginning,

"O kine no longer mine. . . ."

and containing grave breaches of Christian philosophy. Mr. Underwood said, "Cows don't go to heaven," to which Mrs. E.C.B. replied, "Well, this one did," and explained poetic license. Mr. Underwood, who in his time had published memorial verses of indeterminate variety, said he still couldn't print this because it was blasphemous and didn't scan, so to mark her displeasure Mrs. E.C.B. unlocked a frame and scattered the Biggs Store ad all over the office. To mark his displeasure, Mr. Underwood drank an enormous slug of cherry wine in her face, swallowed it down, and cursed her all the way to the courthouse square. After that, instead of having them appear in the *Maycomb County Tribune*, Mrs. E.C.B. had her works published privately by a firm in Tuscaloosa. The county felt the loss.

"You know—"

She came down from the ceiling.

"You know, they had the same kind of spirit we were raised on. That's why I can't get enough of them," Talbert was saying. "Especially when I'm stuck off up there at Northwestern. People don't seem to have much human nature up there—they're not like us."

"It seems to me," she said, making a feeble last-ditch stand, "that if you were homesick you'd naturally turn to Faulkner or somebody."

"I find Faulkner completely unreal."

What he saw in her face made him smile. His smile broadened into a grin and he rubbed the left side of his nose with his right forefinger.

Lord, she thought, he has even acquired their gestures. "More coffee, Talbert?" she said.

"Yes, please."

As she went toward the kitchen, she stopped in the door, turned around, and said, "Talbert, do you by any chance play golf?"

"Why, yes."

She washed and dried the cups, put on a fresh pot of coffee, and while she waited for it to come to a boil, she wondered why she had ever doubted that all things happen for the best in this, the best of all possible worlds.

Essays *and* Miscellaneous Pieces

LOVE—IN OTHER WORDS

Vogue, April 15, 1961

MANY YEARS AGO AN AGING member of the House of Hanover, on learning that the duty of providing an heir to the throne of England had suddenly befallen him and his brothers, confided his alarm to his friend Thomas Creevey: ". . . It is now seven-and-twenty years that Madame St. Laurent and I have lived together; we are of the same age and have been in all climates, and in all difficulties together, and you may well imagine the pang it will occasion me to part with her. . . . I protest I don't know what is to become of her if a marriage is to be forced upon me. . . ."

Amused by the Duke of Kent's predicament, Mr. Creevey recorded the incident in his diary and preserved for us a timeless declaration. The man who made it was not overly endowed with brilliance, nor had he led a noteworthy life, yet we remember his cry from the heart and tend to forget his ultimate service to mankind: he was the father of Queen Victoria.

What did the Duke of Kent tell us? That two people had shared their lives on a voluntary basis for nearly thirty years—in itself a remarkable achievement; that they had survived the fevers and frets of intimate relationship; that together they had met the pressures and disappointments of life; that he is in agony at the prospect of leaving her. In one graceful sentence, the Duke of Kent said all there is to say about the love of a man for a woman.

And in so saying, he tells us much about love itself. There is only one kind of love—love. But the different manifestations of love are uncountable:

At an unfamiliar night noise a mother will spring from bed, not to return until every corner of her domain is tucked safely round her anxiety. A man will look up from his golf game to watch a jet cut caterpillar tracks through the sky. A housewife, before driving to town, will give her neighbor a quick call to see if she wants anything from the store. These are manifestations of a power within us that must of necessity be called divine, for it is no invention of man.

What is love? Many things are like love—indeed, love is present in pity, compassion, romance, affection. What made the Duke of Kent's statement a declaration of love, and what makes us perform without second thought small acts of love every day of our lives, is an element conspicuous by its absence. Were it present, the Duke of Kent would have left his mistress without a pang; the sound barrier breaking over her head would not rouse the mother; sinking his putt would be the primary aim of the golfer; the housewife would go straight to the store with no thought of her neighbor. One thing identifies love and isolates it from kindred emotions: love admits not of self.

Few of us achieve compassion; to some of us romance is a word; in many of us the ability to feel affection has long since died; but all of us at one time or another—be it for an instant or for our lives—have departed from ourselves: we have loved something or someone. Love, then, is a paradox: to have it, we must give it. Love is not an intransitive thing—love is a direct action of mind and body.

Without love, life is pointless and dangerous. Man is on his way to Venus, but he still hasn't learned to live with his wife. Man has succeeded in increasing his life span, yet he exterminates his brothers six million at a whack. Man now has the power to destroy himself and his planet: depend upon it, he will—should he cease to love.

The most common barriers to love are greed, envy, pride, and four other drives formerly known as sins. There is one more just as dangerous: boredom. The mind that can find little excitement in life is a dying one; the mind that cannot find something in the world that attracts it is dead, and the body housing it might as well be dead, for what are the uses of the five senses to a mind that takes no pleasure in them?

Having at long last realized that he must love or destroy himself, man is proceeding along his usual course by trying to evolve a science for it. The ultimate aim of psychoanalysis, when its special brand of semantics is put to rout, is to release man from his neuroses and thus enable him to love, and man's capacity to love is measured by his degree of freedom from the drives that turn inward upon him. As one holds down a cork to the bottom of a stream, so may love be imprisoned by self: remove self, and love rises to the surface of man's being.

With love, all things are possible.

Love restores. We have heard many tales of love's power to heal, and we are skeptical of them, for we are human and therefore prone to deny the existence of things we do not understand and cannot explain. But this tale happened:

On an August evening in a tiny Southern hospital, an old man lay dying. His family had been summoned, among them his eldest grandson, a boy of sixteen. The boy's relationship with his grandfather had been a curious, almost wordless one, as such things often are between man and man. All that day the boy said nothing. It seemed that he could not talk. He would not wait out the old man's dying with the rest of his family in the hospital lobby; instead, the boy found a chair and stationed himself in the corridor beside his grandfather's door, where he sat all day, oblivious to the starched scurryings of hospital routine. Late in the evening the family's doctor found the boy still sitting, still silent. The doctor said, "Go home, son. There's nothing you can do for your grandfather." The boy took no notice of him, and the doctor went into the room only to emerge moments later, looking bewildered. "Er—son," said the doctor. The boy looked up. "He's asking for something to eat. He's better." Showing no sign of surprise, the boy nodded: "I reckoned it was about time he was hungry," he said, his first utterance of the day. Then he picked up the chair, put it back where he found it, and walked down the corridor, stretching his lanky frame and yawning. "Where are you going, boy?" called the doctor. "To get him a hamburger," answered the boy. "He likes hamburgers."

There is no satisfactory explanation for extrasensory perception—it simply is. There was no rational explanation for the old man's recovery—it simply happened. One may only wonder.

Love transforms. Why is it that the quotation we are seeking, when we can't find it in the Bible or in Shakespeare, most often turns up in *Don Quixote*? Because Cervantes, from sheer love of life, made the nuances of life immortal. Why, when we are familiar with every line, must we still stop and listen when the *Messiah* is playing? Because every note was born of a man's love for his God, and we hear it. Try this experiment: catch (if you can) someone who loathes baroque music; play for him any part of *Semele*, then sit back and watch his polite attention turn to compulsive attention—see your captive become Handel's captive. Avarice never wrote a good novel; hate did not paint *The Birth of Venus*; nor did envy reveal to us that the square of the hypotenuse is equal to the sum of the squares of the two sides. Every creation of man's mind that has withstood the buffeting of time was born of love—love of something or someone. It is possible even to love mathematics.

The history of mankind contains innumerable testaments to the power of love, but none touches the transformation undergone by the otherwise cantankerous St. Paul when he addressed himself to the subject: loving, he wrote of love itself, and he gave us a miracle. Listen:

"Though I speak with the tongues of men and of angels, and have not charity, I am become as sounding brass, or a tinkling cymbal.

"And though I have the gift of prophecy, and understand all mysteries, and all knowledge; and though I have all faith, so that I could remove mountains, and have not charity, I am nothing. . . ."

After St. Paul, we have done our best, but our best has never come near him.

Love purifies. Suffering never purified anybody; suffering merely intensifies the self-directed drives within us. Any act of love, however—no matter how small—lessens anxiety's grip, gives us a taste of tomorrow, and eases the yoke of our fears. Love, unlike virtue, is not its own reward. The reward of love is peace of mind, and peace of mind is the end of man's desiring.

CRACKLING

BREAD

The Artists' & Writers' Cookbook, 1961

FIRST, CATCH YOUR PIG. THEN ship it to the *abattoir* nearest you. Bake what they send back. Remove the solid fat and throw the rest away. Fry fat, drain off liquid grease, and combine the residue (called "cracklings") with:

1 ½ cups water-ground white meal

1 teaspoon salt

1 teaspoon baking powder

1 egg

1 cup milk

Bake in very hot oven until brown (about 15 minutes).

Result: one pan crackling bread serving 6. Total cost: about $250, depending upon size of pig. Some historians say by this recipe alone fell the Confederacy.

CHRISTMAS

to ME

McCall's, December 1961

SEVERAL YEARS AGO, I WAS living in New York and working for an airline, so I never got home to Alabama for Christmas—if, indeed, I got the day off. To a displaced Southerner, Christmas in New York can be a rather melancholy occasion, not because the scene is strange to one far from home, but because it is familiar: New York shoppers evince the same singleness of purpose as slow-moving Southerners; Salvation Army bands and Christmas carols are alike the world over; at that time of year, New York streets shine wet with the same gentle farmer's rain that soaks Alabama's winter fields.

I missed Christmas away from home, I thought. What I really missed was a memory, an old memory of people long since gone, of my grandparents' house bursting with cousins, smilax, and holly. I missed the sound of hunting boots, the sudden open-door gusts of chilly air that cut through the aroma of pine needles and oyster dressing. I missed my brother's night-before-Christmas mask of rectitude and my father's bumblebee bass humming "Joy to the World."

In New York, I usually spent the day, or what was left of it, with my closest friends in Manhattan. They were a young family in periodically well-to-do circumstances. Periodically, because the head of the household employed the precarious craft of writing for their living. He was brilliant and lively; his one defect of character was an inordinate love of puns. He possessed a trait curious not only in a writer but in a young man with dependents: there was about him a quality of fearless optimism—not of the wishing-makes-it-so variety, but that of seeing an attainable goal and daring to take risks in its pursuit. His audacity sometimes left his friends breathless—who in his circumstances would venture to buy a town house in Manhattan? His shrewd generalship made the undertaking successful; while most young people are content to dream of such things, he made his dream a reality for his family and satisfied his tribal longing for his own ground beneath his feet. He had come to New York from the Southwest and, in a manner characteristic of the natives thereof, had found the most beautiful girl in the East and promptly married her.

To this ethereal, utterly feminine creature were born two strapping sons, who, as they grew, discovered that their fragile mother packed a wallop that was second to nobody's. Her capacity to love was enormous, and she spent hours in her kitchen, producing dark, viscous delights for her family and her friends.

They were a handsome pair, healthy in mind and body,

happy in their extremely active lives. Common interests as well as love drew me to them: an endless flow of reading material circulated amongst us; we took pleasure in the same theater, films, music; we laughed at the same things, and we laughed so much in those days.

Our Christmases together were simple. We limited our gifts to pennies and wits and all-out competition. Who would come up with the most outrageous for the least? The real Christmas was for the children, an idea that I found totally compatible, for I had long ago ceased to speculate on the meaning of Christmas as anything other than a day for children. Christmas to me was only a memory of old loves and empty rooms, something I buried with the past that underwent a vague, aching resurrection once every year.

One Christmas, though, was different. I was lucky. I had the whole day off, and I spent Christmas Eve with them. When morning came, I awoke to a small hand kneading my face. "Dup," was all its owner had time to say. I got downstairs just in time to see the little boys' faces as they beheld the pocket rockets and space equipment Santa Claus had left them. At first, their fingers went almost timidly over their toys. When their inspection had been completed, the two boys dragged everything into the center of the living room.

Bedlam prevailed until they discovered that there was

more. As their father began distributing gifts, I grinned to myself, wondering how my exceptionally wily unearthments this year would be received. His was a print of a portrait of Sydney Smith I'd found for thirty-five cents; hers was the complete works of Margot Asquith, the result of a year's patient search. The children were in agonies of indecision over which package to open next, and as I waited, I noticed that while a small stack of presents mounted beside their mother's chair, I had received not a single one. My disappointment was growing steadily, but I tried not to show it.

They took their time. Finally she said, "We haven't forgotten you. Look on the tree."

There was an envelope on the tree, addressed to me. I opened it and read: "You have one year off from your job to write whatever you please. Merry Christmas."

"What does this mean?" I asked.

"What it says," I was told.

They assured me that it was not some sort of joke. They'd had a good year, they said. They'd saved some money and thought it was high time they did something about me.

"What do you mean, do something about me?"

To tell the truth—if I really wanted to know—they thought I had a great talent, and—

"What makes you think that?"

It was plain to anyone who knew me, they said, if anyone would stop to look. They wanted to show their faith in me the best way they knew how. Whether I ever sold a line was immaterial. They wanted to give me a full, fair chance to learn my craft, free from the harassments of a regular job. Would I accept their gift? There were no strings at all. Please accept, with their love.

It took some time to find my voice. When I did, I asked if they were out of their minds. What made them think anything would come of this? They didn't have that kind of money to throw away. A year was a long time. What if the children came down with something horrible? As objection crowded upon objection, each was overruled. "We're all young," they said. "We can cope with whatever happens. If disaster strikes, you can always find a job of some kind. Okay, consider it a loan, then, if you wish. We just want you to accept. Just permit us to believe in you. You must."

"It's a fantastic gamble," I murmured. "It's such a great risk."

My friend looked around his living room, at his boys, half buried under a pile of bright Christmas wrapping paper. His eyes sparkled as they met his wife's, and they exchanged a glance of what seemed to me insufferable smugness. Then he looked at me and said softly, "No, honey. It's not a risk. It's a sure thing."

Outside, snow was falling, an odd event for a New York Christmas. I went to the window, stunned by the day's miracle. Christmas trees blurred softly across the street, and firelight made the children's shadows dance on the wall beside me. A full, fair chance for a new life. Not given me by an act of generosity, but by an act of love. *Our faith in you* was really all I had heard them say. I would do my best not to fail them. Snow still fell on the pavement below. Brownstone roofs gradually whitened. Lights in distant skyscrapers shone with yellow symbols of a road's lonely end, and as I stood at the window, looking at the lights and the snow, the ache of an old memory left me forever.

GREGORY PECK

Special Program from
the American Film Institute, 1989

WHEN I ARRIVED IN CALIFORNIA to watch the first week's filming of *To Kill a Mockingbird*, I was not in a state of complete innocence. Having been acquainted with the work of the producer, director, screenwriter and star, I knew that the novel was in good hands. All were gifted, consummate professionals.

I was fascinated by the way things are done on a studio lot. A small-town, Southern neighborhood, vintage Early Depression, was being assembled, and I was shown how some of the houses would serve a dual purpose. On-camera they would comprise Maycomb, Alabama. Off-camera they would serve as dressing-rooms for the actors, plus a schoolroom for the children in the cast.

As I watched the crew bring in huge trees and set them in place, the director said, "We need a knot-hole in that one."

"I've got one at home," said the assistant director. "I'll bring it tomorrow."

When I was taken to a sound stage, I found reproduced, on a much smaller scale, the courtroom from my own hometown in Alabama. Exactly right in every detail, but I pointed out that Gregory Peck at 6'4" would scrape the balcony.

When I looked into the camera, though, the courtroom had somehow grown larger to fit the people in it.

Portable knot-holes, expanding courtrooms—all in a day's magic.

At the wardrobe tests, as the actors walked past the camera, I marveled that the cast had been so carefully chosen; they looked so nearly like my own vision of the characters. Great so far, but what about Atticus? As I pondered, the front door of the Finch house opened, and he appeared.

A light summer suit, watch-chain across vest, a straw hat and horn-rimmed glasses, a lithe, still-youthful Gregory Peck had somehow grown heavier and solidly into his fifties. The illusion was complete.

As complete as could meet the eye. When filming began, I was relieved to hear that the non-natives in the cast had made no special attempt at Southern accents. Nothing empties a Southern movie house faster than tin-eared actors. Gregory Peck was showing admirable restraint. In rehearsal and in the few scenes I watched with the camera rolling, he permitted himself one harmless indulgence, an unobtrusive Southern *you*. There was a lesson here for all young screenwriters—when spoken, lines written in implacable Southern idiom create the illusion of Southern voices.

I left California feeling fortunate indeed. A great cast, a great director, a screenplay that was a work of art in itself. A group of highly intelligent professionals who respected my work—what more could any novelist hope for?

I hoped for no more. Later in the year when I saw the completed film, I got a surprise that remains one of the high points of my life.

I watched an inspired performance.

In some mysterious way, Gregory Peck's Atticus Finch transcended illusion.

Actors are reluctant to give away their trade secrets. With the passage of time, with more than twenty-five years of his friendship, the mystery of that performance has steadily unfolded, to my great reward and on-going delight. I know what Gregory Peck, gifted and consummate professional, brought to the part—he included himself.

WHEN CHILDREN DISCOVER AMERICA

McCall's, August 1965

WORDSWORTH WAS RIGHT WHEN HE said that we trail clouds of glory as we come into the world, that we are born with a divine sense of perception. As we grow older, the world closes in on us, and we gradually lose the freshness of viewpoint that we had as children. That is why I think children should get to know this country while they are young.

I do not think the youngest or even the most jaded citizen could go to Washington and through the Capitol or the Smithsonian Institution without having the feeling of yes, we *are* something; yes, we *do* have a history. It may be a short one, but every bit of it has worked to make us what we are, and it's there to be felt in Washington.

I would take children to the South, perhaps to Charleston, a small city of great character and great historic interest—a seaport town with a distinct air of something that *was*. In the Far West I would show children San Francisco. The Chinese people there are *such* wonderful Americans. They are people with their own ancient culture, and yet they have become part of our civilization. New England, of course—in autumn, you can get drunk on maple trees. And that first sight of the Rockies from the plains in Colorado. You go through miles and miles of flatland country—and then suddenly, there they are, snow-capped in all their majesty. Oceans and beaches . . . the Gulf side of Florida, down around Naples and Sarasota, with green, green water. And my own part of home—pine-forest country, dense and beautiful.

I would like to show children my own town, my own street, my own neighbors. I live on the corner. My next-door neighbor is a barber, and his wife owns a dress shop. My down-the-street neighbor has a grocery store, and my neighbor down the hill is a teacher. My neighbor to the rear is a doctor; behind him is a druggist. If children were visiting—from abroad or from other parts of the country—they would have cookies and ice cream for them, and take them to the park with the lake and the swimming pool, and my cook, Mary, would make them an enormous cake covered with caramel frosting, and for dinner give them fresh vegetables from the garden and Southern chicken cooked right.

And then we would let them alone, to explore on their own. It's stifling to have adults with you all the time when you are a child, to tell you about everything and explain things away for you. There is no sense of discovery for a young, exploring spirit when adults are with you all the time to give absolutely straight answers to everything.

I don't think, for instance, that the Lincoln Memorial needs to be pointed out to any human being of any age. I would let children discover the beauty and mystery and grandeur of it. They'll ask questions later. No child can possibly leave the Lincoln Memorial without questions, often important questions.

If more young people traveled with their eyes and minds open and saw this country, they would have a deeper feeling about it. Adventuring across the country is out of style. Whatever happened to working after school in a grocery store to get enough money to hitchhike to California during your vacation? My youngest nephew may be one of the last to do that, and he did it when he was fifteen. His parents were terrified, but he got himself to the World's Fair. His mother had thoughtfully sewn a bus ticket into the cuff of his trousers, but he swore he would never use it. He ended up in Chicago and lived on milk and rolls for three days because he didn't have any money. When he finally got home, he had lost thirty pounds; but he was the happiest boy I had ever seen in my life. He had discovered America for himself. It will mean something to him for the rest of his life.

Younger children may not respond in words, but they will drink everything in with their eyes, and fill their minds with awareness and wonder. It's an experience they will enjoy and remember all their lives; and it will give them greater pride in their own country.

TRUMAN CAPOTE

Book of the Month Club Newsletter,
January 1966

ON A CHILLY FALL DAY in 1959 Truman Capote set out for Kansas armed with a footlocker of comestibles sufficient to support a few weeks of life in that forbidding land, little knowing that he was to devote the next five years to a work infinitely tantalizing and a true challenge to his genius.

At first it was like being on another planet: a vast terrain indifferent to the creatures that walked upon it, an untrusting populace suspicious of anyone alien to it, bone-cracking winters turning to dust-choked springs to parching summers. Nevertheless, in the due course of time Truman became as much a fixture to Finney County, Kansas, as are the roadside signs proclaiming its many virtues.

What he found in Kansas is on the pages of *In Cold Blood*. What did Kansas find in Truman Capote? To begin with, looks that are deceiving. One sees a beautifully modeled head, sensitive hands, a graceful carriage, blue eyes behind thick glasses. One's impression is suddenly modified by the casual strength his handshake conveys, and rightly so, for beneath the elegant lines of his suit are hidden a hard body and the stamina of ten battalions.

When one encounters his tough-mindedness first impressions fade altogether: here is an acute intelligence, a highly trained sense of observation, an intuition that makes accurate assessments with lightning speed. If one is conscious of an impersonal gaze, one is equally aware of total commitment and single-minded sense of purpose—qualities shared, oddly enough, by criminals and geniuses.

Truman was born in New Orleans in 1924, and after an unhappy, nomadic childhood published his first work at the age of 16—not surprising when one considers that he began writing the moment he began reading. As a child Truman was interested in little else. It was then that he developed the vocation, the disciplines of language and self necessary to his art; he was born with the rest. He produced his first novel (unhappily lost to posterity) at the age of 10.

He never really had a childhood: his astonishing intelligence was mistaken for foolishness; his boredom with formal education was thought to be listlessness; his insatiable interest in human motivations was called unhealthy curiosity. But he kept his own counsel and in his apartness he quietly pursued his craft. Over the years Truman made himself the master of any literary form he chose to employ.

He is a short-story writer of the first rank: "Miriam" is

already a classic. He was 23 years old when *Other Voices, Other Rooms* established his reputation as a novelist. Then followed (not necessarily in this order) more short stories, a joyous adventure in screen writing called *Beat the Devil*, the musical play *House of Flowers*, *The Muses Are Heard* and *Breakfast at Tiffany's*, among other works. All are different, each is stamped with the same sensibility and craftsmanship.

He is a born wanderer. Since adulthood he has lived in various parts of the world—France, Haiti, Italy, Sicily, Africa, Greece, Russia, Switzerland. Always sensitive to his surroundings, Truman first settled down on the western plains with the wryness of General Grant: he proposed to fight it out on that line if it took all summer. It took longer.

In addition to receiving his literary gifts with sometimes maddening innocence, rural Kansas made the pleasant discovery that Truman Capote's personal characteristics are accented by an irrepressible capacity for enjoyment. He is never bored and is never boring. His conversation is astringent; his mordant wit softens into easy laughter. He likes nothing better than to split the landscape in fast sports cars. When given the opportunity he will swim a mile out into the ocean. He plays jazz records loudly and with no encouragement will perform a twist of his own invention called I'm Beside Myself. He seldom goes to films, but when he does he will see three in one day. He likes to be comfortable; he collects antique paperweights; his household includes a fat bulldog and a thin cat, both travelers, both spoiled.

When its inhabitants drew close enough for a less superficial inspection, Kansas found him to be, in spirit, an aristocrat: Truman pursues excellence; he suffers fools only when necessary; he is impatient of bad taste and cannot tolerate mediocrity in writing or in people. By instinct he is a democrat—his friends come from every station in life and speak in a bewildering variety of tongues. People always react sharply to his presence, sometimes with stirrings of envy, most often with the feeling that when he comes into their lives he gives them his best.

For over five years Truman Capote gave Kansas his best—identification complete, involvement total. His task was epic: the material he assembled in the course of his labor is the size of a sand hill (in Kansas, a modest mountain). His sense of estrangement was at first acute, but slowly, with infinite patience, he wove himself into the fabric of the country, becoming at one with the land and looking with his unique gifts into many hearts.

Kansans will spend the rest of their days at the tantalizing game of discovering Truman; what Truman found in Kansans will make people everywhere discover themselves.

ROMANCE

and

HIGH ADVENTURE

Lecture Delivered at the 1983
Alabama History and Heritage Festival;
published in *Clearings in the Thicket:
An Alabama Humanities Reader*, 1985

ALBERT JAMES PICKETT WAS BORN in 1810, in Anson County, North Carolina, and moved with his family to what is now Autauga County, Alabama, in 1818, where his father established a plantation and trading-house. He received a "gentleman's education," which meant a military academy in Connecticut and Stafford County Academy in Virginia. In 1830 he returned home. Although he acquired extensive acreage in the vicinity of his father's plantation, Pickett was no farmer. Agriculture, he said, "did not occupy one-fourth of my time. Having no taste for politics, and never having studied a profession, I determined to write a history." It was lucky for us that he did.

After spending more than seventeen years collecting the material, Pickett began writing his *History of Alabama* in 1847. It was published in 1851 and, after having gone through several editions to 1900, was out of print until 1962, when it was republished as a sort of historical curiosity.

We Americans like to put our culture into disposable containers. Nowhere is this more evident than in the way we treat our past. We discard villages, towns, even cities, when they grow old, and we are now in the process of discarding our recorded history, not in a shredder, but by rewriting it as romance. We are eager to watch docu-dramas on television; we prefer to read a history of the American Revolution as seen through the eyes of Mad Anthony Wayne's last mistress. Now there is nothing wrong in reading historical fiction—perhaps two-thirds of the world's classics are written in that form. But these are impatient days; more than ever it seems that we want anything but the real thing: we are afraid that the real thing might be dull, demanding, and worst of all, lacking in suspense.

So it gives me the greatest pleasure to remind the members of my own generation (who have all read it) and report to the younger ones among us, that although it's the real thing, Pickett's *History of Alabama* is a work so fraught with romance and high adventure that even John Jakes would sit up and take notice.

In what would occupy a few paragraphs of an American history survey, Pickett took 669 pages to unfold a story that is more hair-raising than anything yet seen on television. Indeed, in today's terms, it is almost as though Pickett trained a camera in relentless, unblinking close-up on a period of Alabama history that we seldom think about any more, a period that sometimes seems to live only in our place-names and on roadside markers. (Where was Maubila? On the Tombigbee somewhere? Where was Tukabatchee? On the

Coosa, or was it the Tallapoosa? Maybe it was on the Alabama. There were the names of separate and distinct peoples, with their own history.)

In a prose style that falls somewhere between Macaulay and Bulwer-Lytton, Pickett's history opens with a bloodcurdling account of Hernando de Soto's progress through our state, in which he destroyed nearly everything in his path, including the Mobilians and their giant chief, Tuscaloosa, the Black Warrior.

Had he been a modern historian, Pickett would have gone straight on from there, but "as our soil remained untrodden by European feet for nearly a century and a half," Pickett passed the time between de Soto and the arrival of the French with five chapters of what makes for compulsive reading. In a long digression describing the native inhabitants of what is now Alabama, Georgia, and Mississippi, he wrote a miniature social history that can hold its own with any modern work. For these chapters alone, I think Pickett deserves a place in American literature.

We meet them all, but the most prominent tribes were the ferocious, insolent Chickasaws, who put paid to de Soto somewhere in Mississippi; the silver-tongued Choctaws, who could not swim, who were unaggressive when not defending their own turf, and who were notable even among their own kind for their revolting burial practices. In the northeast were the comparatively genial Cherokees, and in the west the aristocratic, despotic Natchez. On center stage were the Muscogees, later known as the Creeks, who, after pushing into the state in the vacuum created by de Soto, formed a confederation with the Alabamas and remnants of the shattered smaller tribes. Pickett's history is essentially the story of the Creeks and the people who destroyed them.

The Creeks were a remarkable people. Their social and political structure was as complex as anything in Europe, and in some ways was far more advanced than that of the earliest settlers. Divorce, for example, was at the choice of either party and with only a slight advantage to the man: He could remarry immediately, but the woman had to wait until The Green Corn Dance was over. "Marriage," said Pickett, "gave no right to the husband over the property of the wife, or the control or management of the children he might have by her." Adultery, however, was another matter. The pains and penalties for that sport rendered its practice infrequent.

They were a gregarious people. "Their most manly and important game was 'the ball play,'" said Pickett; it seemed to be a version of lacrosse. The warriors of one town challenged those of another, and "for several days previous to the time, those who intended to engage in the amusement took medicine, as though they were going to war." In the presence of multitudes, the players "rushed together with a mighty shock . . . were often severely hurt, and sometimes killed, in the rough and unfeeling scramble which prevailed. . . . In the meantime, the women were constantly on the alert with vessels and gourds filled with water, watching every opportunity to supply the players. It sometimes happened that the inhabitants of a town gamed away all their ponies, jewels, and wearing apparel. . . ." Does that sound familiar? Every fall and winter weekend finds today's Alabamians at similar pursuits.

Their religion, an integral part of everything that they did, was so complicated and structured as to delight the heart of a pharisee. Indeed, Pickett delights *us* with the theories of one James Adair, who lived among the Indians for more than thirty years and emerged from the forest in 1775 with an enormous volume that sought to prove that the Creeks and their neighbors were in fact Jews. After observing the intricate similarities of the two religions, the clincher for Adair was in watching the warriors dance "around the holy fire, during which the elder priest invoked the Great Spirit, while the others responded *Hallelu! Hallelu!* then *Halleluiah! Halleluiah!*"

Pickett's narrative of the sufferings, struggles, and massacres of the early colonists, the gradual opening of the region to commerce, the various wars and alliances of the three greedy powers—Britain, France, and Spain—is one of fascinating detail. We follow the fortunes of the Sieur de Bienville, who must have been appointed governor of the French colony by mistake, because he was a decent, incorruptible and, on the whole, benevolent man. Along the way we meet the English General James Oglethorpe and his philanthropical experiment in Georgia, and incidentally get a glimpse of John and Charles Wesley. We meet schemers, rogues, and vagabonds; scores of minor characters come alive on the pages—one elegant lady on the razzle in the wilderness, claiming to be the Tsar of Russia's sister-in-law; the valiant Beaudrot, for whom many Southerners are named, but don't know exactly why; the Jewish trader Abram Mordecai, who spent fifty years in the wilderness and had his ear cut off for amorous dalliance with a married squaw.

Through the years, when the Indians felt too much pressure from the constant encroachments of the Europeans, they always responded to broken promises with savage violence, until there appeared among the Creeks their greatest chieftain, Alexander McGillivray, who led them to the high-watermark of their history. The story of McGillivray and his family should be so familiar to all Alabamians that

I shall not repeat it, but say that if the Creeks ever had a chance to survive as a nation, they had it with him. Yet in the seventeen years of his spectacular leadership, McGillivray showed his feet of clay—his intrigues with the brand-new American government and with the Spanish authorities in Florida, for his personal aggrandizement, set the Creeks on a collision course with extinction.

The Indians hated the new Americans even more than they hated the British, French, and Spanish—there were more of them. The second Yazoo Land Sale (the first was a fizzle) resulted in more settlers coming in as never before—this time under the protection of the American government.

The Americans established outposts and small forts on Alabama's rivers, cleared the forests, and gradually created a recognizable society in the wilderness, sometimes marrying the descendants of the first settlers who had married Indians. Many of the oldest families in Alabama can proudly point to their Indian heritage.

Now a note of warning—when we think of Alabama history we think of slavery and we should. In 1540 when de Soto arrived with his slaves, he found the Indians enslaving each other; when the French first imported African slaves, the Africans were bought by prosperous Indians or captured as prizes in raids. In 1847 when Pickett began to write his history, slavery was a fact of life and he treats it as such, so don't be shocked. Slavery, you still remember, is man's oldest institution, and its abolition is the only fundamental moral change that Western man has yet made.

Well, just when everybody was settling in and government agents were helping manage Indian affairs, the United States and Britain went to war. The Indians had given permission for the new Federal Road to cut through the heart of their territory, which meant even more emigrants, and the Creeks, said Pickett, "with their usual sagacity, foresaw that they would soon be hemmed in by the Georgians on one side and the Tombigbee people on the other." The Spanish to the south hated the emigrants also. British agents, operating in Canada and as guests of the Spanish in Pensacola, urged the Creeks to come in on their side against the Americans, and from Detroit they sent to Alabama an evangelist I can only describe as a direct ancestor of the Ayatollah Khomeini.

Chief Tecumseh, a Shawnee of national renown as a warrior, and his chief prophet descended upon Creek villages preaching fire and revolution. Pickett's description of their performance at the Creek capital, Tukabatchee, at a grand council of the Indians, is spine-chilling. Here is a summary of Tecumseh's remarks: return to your primitive customs; throw away the plough and the loom; become warriors again; stay away from the grasping unprincipled white race; when they've cut down your beautiful forests and stained your clear rivers, they will subject you to African servitude; dress again in the skins of beasts, use the war club, the scalping knife, and the bow; drive them out and destroy them.

Tecumseh's chief prophet was also busy. He established a soothsaying college and turned out local prophets trained in new and potent magic. Although the rank and file drank the magic brew eagerly, the Big Warrior at Tukabatchee was skeptical. Tecumseh said, "You do not mean to fight. I know the reason. You do not believe the Great Spirit has sent me. You shall believe it. . . . I shall go straight to Detroit. When I get there I will stamp my foot upon the ground and shake down every house in Tukabatchee."

The common Indians, said Pickett, believed every word of Tecumseh's threat, and they counted the days it took Tecumseh to reach Detroit. "One day," said Pickett, "a mighty rumbling was heard in the earth, the houses of Tukabatchee reeled and tottered, and reeled again." As if a fortuitous earthquake were not enough, the British at Pensacola provided a further incentive to war: they offered the Indians $10 a scalp.

The Red Sticks—the war party, the fundamentalists—went on the rampage throughout Alabama. Creek families were divided (not the least of which was the family of Alexander McGillivray) and they fought each other as well as the Americans. It was not until after the massacre at Fort Mims, led by McGillivray's nephew, William Weatherford, that help came from the north.

Andrew Jackson with his Tennesseans at Talladega and General Claiborne in the south at the Holy Ground—where, incidentally, Alexander McGillivray's sister was found tied to a stake surrounded by a lightwood fire, and where her nephew, Weatherford, who had put her there, made his famous escape—were engagements that began to spell the end, which came, as we all know, in a few furious hours at Horseshoe Bend in Tallapoosa County.

Tecumseh's revival meeting at Tukabatchee resulted in the Creeks losing nearly one-half of what is now Alabama, and their eventual removal from the state.

Pickett ended his history with the admission of Alabama to the Union in 1819. "To some other person," he said, "fonder than we are of the dry details of state legislation and fierce party spirit, we leave the task of bringing the history down to a later period."

But I wonder if that was his reason. I think Pickett left his heart at Horseshoe Bend. I do not believe that it was in him to write of the eventual fate of the Creek Nation, of the

Cherokees, of the Chickasaws and Choctaws which was decided well within his own lifetime.

Pickett's *History of Alabama*, this unique treasure, now lies hidden in old family bookcases, has been discarded by libraries, sometimes turns up in rummage sales, and is certainly not used in our schools. In my opinion it should be in every high school library in the state.

I have no idea what today's historians think of Albert Pickett—very little, I should guess, for Pickett's history is composed of small dramas within a huge drama, much of it drawn from the memories of those who were there, from individuals whose bravery and sacrifice created the state of Alabama. Modern research techniques and professionally objective evaluations were unknown to Pickett, as they were unknown to his contemporaries Macaulay and Prescott, but then who reads them any more?

A

LETTER *from*

HARPER LEE

O, The Oprah Magazine,
July 2006

May 7, 2006

Dear Oprah,

Do you remember when you learned to read, or like me, can you not even remember a time when you didn't know how? I must have learned from having been read to by my family. My sisters and brother, much older, read aloud to keep me from pestering them; my mother read me a story every day, usually a children's classic, and my father read from the four newspapers he got through every evening. Then, of course, it was Uncle Wiggily at bedtime.

So I arrived in the first grade, literate, with a curious cultural assimilation of American history, romance, the Rover Boys, Rapunzel, and *The Mobile Press*. Early signs of genius? Far from it. Reading was an accomplishment I shared with several local contemporaries. Why this endemic precocity? Because in my hometown, a remote village in the early 1930s, youngsters had little to do but read. A movie? Not often—movies weren't for small children. A park for games? Not a hope. We're talking unpaved streets here, and the Depression.

Books were scarce. There was nothing you could call a public library, we were a hundred miles away from a department store's books section, so we children began to circulate reading material among ourselves until each child had read another's entire stock. There were long dry spells broken by the new Christmas books, which started the rounds again.

As we grew older, we began to realize what our books were worth: *Anne of Green Gables* was worth two Bobbsey Twins; two Rover Boys were an even swap for two Tom Swifts. Aesthetic frissons ran a poor second to the thrills of acquisition. The goal, a full set of a series, was attained only once by an individual of exceptional greed—he swapped his sister's doll buggy.

We were privileged. There were children, mostly from rural areas, who had never looked into a book until they went to school. They had to be taught to read in the first grade, and we were impatient with them for having to catch up. We ignored them.

And it wasn't until we were grown, some of us, that we discovered what had befallen the children of our African-American servants. In some of their schools, pupils learned to read three-to-one—three children to one book, which was more than likely a cast-off primer from a white grammar school. We seldom saw them until, older, they came to work for us.

Now, 75 years later in an abundant society where people have laptops, cell phones, iPods, and minds like empty rooms, I still plod along with books. Instant information is not for me. I prefer to search library stacks because when I work to learn something, I remember it.

And, Oprah, can you imagine curling up in bed to read a computer? Weeping for Anna Karenina and being terrified by Hannibal Lecter, entering the heart of darkness with Mistah Kurtz, having Holden Caulfield ring you up—some things should happen on soft pages, not cold metal.

The village of my childhood is gone, with it most of the book collectors, including the dodgy one who swapped his complete set of Seckatary Hawkinses for a shotgun and kept it until it was retrieved by an irate parent.

Now we are three in number and live hundreds of miles away from each other. We still keep in touch by telephone conversations of recurrent theme: "What is your name again?" followed by "What are you reading?"

We don't always remember.

Much love,

Harper

SOURCES *for the* ESSAYS *and* MISCELLANEOUS PIECES

"Love—in Other Words," *Vogue*, April 15, 1961, 64–5.

"Crackling Bread," *The Artists' & Writers' Cookbook*, 1961, 251–2.

"Christmas to Me," *McCall's*, December 1961, 63.

Essay on Gregory Peck, special program from the American Film Institute, 1989, 10–11.

"When Children Discover America," *McCall's*, August 1965, 77.

Essay on Truman Capote, newsletter of the Book of the Month Club, January 1966, 6–7.

"Romance and High Adventure," *Clearings in the Thicket: An Alabama Humanities Reader: Essays and Stories from the 1983 Alabama History and Heritage Festival*, ed. Jerry Elijah Brown (Mercer University Press, 1985), 13–20.

"A Letter from Harper Lee," *O, The Oprah Magazine*, July 2006, 151–3.

ABOUT THE AUTHOR

HARPER LEE was born in 1926 in Monroeville, Alabama. She is the author of the acclaimed *To Kill a Mockingbird*, originally published in 1960; and *Go Set a Watchman*, published in July 2015. Ms Lee received the Pulitzer Prize, the Presidential Medal of Freedom, and numerous other literary awards and honours. She died in 2016.

CASEY CEP is at work on the authorized biography of Harper Lee. A staff writer at the *New Yorker*, she is the author of the bestselling book *Furious Hours: Murder, Fraud, and the Last Trial of Harper Lee*. She was born and raised on the Eastern Shore of Maryland, where she still lives with her family.

An Essay by Dr. Edwin Lee Conner, Nephew of Harper Lee

I WAS BORN IN EUFAULA, ALABAMA, in 1947, and I visited my aunt, Nelle Harper Lee, virtually every summer in Monroeville, where she lived part-time with my Aunt Alice; my grandfather A.C. Lee, the model for Atticus; and my Lee cousins, Molly and Ed, the children of Nelle's brother, Ed, the model for Jem. In later years, I saw my aunt a number of times in New York City before she returned to Monroeville toward the end of her life.

The family all knew that she had left Alabama for New York City in the 1940s because she wanted to be a published writer, and that she was following the example of her childhood friend Truman Capote. We were aware that she had been working on stories and then a novel, though she was reluctant to say much more about her writing to us or to anyone else, to my knowledge. My mother, Louise Lee Conner, knew before *To Kill a Mockingbird* was published that she had completed a novel entitled *Go Set a Watchman*. In later years we knew that she had written short stories, and we even knew the names of some of them, though we had no idea if they still existed. When they were discovered among the large accumulation of books and papers that she left behind in her apartment, we were delighted. This book is the result of that discovery.

In the politically polarized culture that we Americans now live in, it is unusual to encounter someone whose experience, understanding, and love for people can embrace different points of view, racial backgrounds, beliefs, opinions, and prejudices. My aunt, Nelle Harper Lee, was such a person, and *To Kill a Mockingbird* has brought that home to many readers. The stories here are full of this empathy. They are deeply autobiographical, and in their narratives about life both in southeast Alabama and in New York City, they illuminate the common humanity that unites people everywhere, South or North, Black or white. I remember the years during which these stories were written, and I can say confidently that they are all rooted in the particular experiences of Nelle's life. I can even identify some of the prototypes for the characters. Scout (as Jean Louise Finch), Atticus (as the lawyer father), and Jem are all here in earlier fictional incarnations—and even Dill, as the adult Truman Capote in a nonfiction piece. There are other members of her family present in these stories, such as her sister Alice, who held the family together when the frailties of the others threatened serious problems.

You will meet an adolescent girl named Abbie, so terrified of her innocent secret being found out that she almost ends it all climbing "the tallest thing in Maiben County" and reaching "The Water Tank." The main character of "The Pinking Shears" is a little girl named Jean Louie (not quite Louise) Finch, whose lawyer father has the dignified manner of Atticus. Three stories set in New York City take us to the Upper East Side neighborhood where Nelle lived—its streets, movie houses, and apartments. We return to Maiben/Maycomb/Monroeville in the last two stories, "The Cat's Meow" and "The Land of Sweet Forever," which feature the home of Nelle's sister Alice after the death of their parents and the move to a new house in a more spacious part of town, just six blocks from the house well-known from the novel and movie of *To Kill a Mockingbird*. These last stories feature narrators who are the barely fictionalized versions of the adult Nelle as she was in her late twenties. I can recall other real people who were the models for characters who appear here, like Arthur of "The Cat's Meow." With the publication of this book, all these fictional characters join the human community of our imaginations, as well as characters we know from her other books. All these characters came alive in Nelle Harper Lee's imagination, and will now come alive in our own. Enjoy them.